TWICE UPON A TIMELINE

TIME CLONES
BOOK 1

BRETT JACKSON

BRETTISH
BOOKS

OTHER BOOKS BY BRETT JACKSON

For more books, please visit the website at

https://www.brettishbooks.com

*This book is dedicated to
my wonderful wife Karen
and our fantastic family.*

*Without your support,
this book would have faded
into the past a long time ago.*

I love you all xx

SPECIAL THANKS

In no particular order.

I would like to say a huge THANK YOU to my friends and family for standing by me and encouraging me to carry on.

Special mentions to Janet and Charlie W, Nicki and Neal G, Jess L, Wayne and Jill A, Sue J, Denise L, Margaret and John S, Sandra E, Barbara and Bob J, Joy, Margaret and Peter V, Ann L, Sherry and Richard F and everyone else who has touched our lives (sorry I couldn't fit you all in).

Thank you also, to Writing Squad on Twitter, and the authors in Next Level Authors, Unstoppable Authors, and Great Writers Share on Facebook. Your input has been invaluable, your company fantastic, and your wisdom has helped so many authors live out their dreams.

And finally, I would like to give a special thank you to best-selling author Daniel Willcocks for his excellent coaching, and motivation to get this book done. His advice and tutoring have been invaluable in the final phases of the production of this novel. Thank you also to the Rebel Author herself Sacha Black and the many wonderful people in Next Level Authors :)

For all of you not mentioned here, thank you for being there for me, and for waiting the five and a half gruelling years it has taken me to write this novel.

And last but most importantly, thanks to you, the reader, for supporting me, and buying this book.

I hope it was worth it. Enjoy reading.

Love and Peace

Brett Jackson.

CHAPTER 1

1 May 2028

Location: Secret Laboratory, Kisterwich

The big wooden door creaked and groaned, and Bob Stafford let out a heavy grunt as it opened. Water dripped onto the slabs as he took off his security guard's cap and hung his waterproof overcoat on the stand.

He was a stocky man, with a crew cut, wearing a brass name badge, pressed white shirt, and black tie and trousers, neatly pressed, which showed the discipline and pride he had earned during his previous career in the army.

Behind him, the large stained-glass windows filled with lightning as the sky lit up with electricity. The brightness of the flash faded, plunging the inside of the Abbey back to darkness, with only the flickering of his torch to show whatever the beam hit. With a firm grip on the wrought iron handle, he pulled the door closed with a satisfying clunk, and turned the key.

As he locked the door, he heard the familiar voices of the Professor and his assistant echoing as they walked up the steps towards him.

"Hi Bull," said Rhea, strolling towards him. She'd always

called him this, ever since he had told her, that it was his nick-name in the service, when the boys noticed his name was Stafford, so they called him Pitbull, then shortened it to bull. It made him sound like someone you didn't want to trifle with, but in reality Bull was a caring sort, and that's why he had enlisted in the army in the role of medic.

"Hey Miss, have you been pulling an all-nighter?"

"Yea, off to get some sleep now," she said, yawning.

"That rain sounds bad," said the Professor listening to the crashing of water against the glass.

"It's not too great, but the wind is worst, nearly blew my cap off," he said, holding it up.

Rhea smiled "Glad you kept hold of it. By the way, ignore the mess in the lab, we will sort it out in the morning."

Bull unlocked the door and opened it. The rain was much heavier now.

"Okey dokey, thanks for letting me know. You look shattered, I'd best let you two get off home."

"Goodnight," said Rhea "Come on Uncle Eric, let's get you home". The Professor yawned as he opened the door and moments later they had gone. Bob locked the massive wooden door.

Looking around the deserted Abbey, he could see the pews, crosses and various other adornments from past blessings, marriages, baptisms and funerals. The vast building had experienced its fair share of action, from its construction in the 1200s to the sieges and many battles, and had the scars to prove it. It had lost its roof twice, the first time in the bombings, and the second time after being hit by lightning. Thankfully, there were safeguards in place to ensure this would never happen again.

The security guard wiped his feet on the large mat and headed for the door to the crypt, the heels of his shiny black shoes clacking on the heavy flagstones. He sat down at the guard's station, put his feet up on the desk, switched on the lamp, glanced at the monitors for signs of movement, and then flipped on the radio.

With only two minutes towards the end of the game, the crowd was getting louder, as the prospect of a goal was becoming close, and the commentator was becoming very excited. Bull leant forward, egging his team on, knowing this was going to be it. The ball went from one player to another, and the crowd got louder as the ball went off the pitch. The commentator gave some history about the replacement who came onto the pitch, and the referee called for a corner shot.

Bob listened intently, he knew this was going to be it. That fifty-to-one bet he had put down was going to make him rich.

"James Sergeant, the new transfer, is throwing the ball in, to Dave Henney who picks it up, he's got control. Henney runs past McKinnon, Walsh and Davis, as Jackson attempts to intercept, and wipes out on the floor. The crowd is going wild. Where is the defence from the other team? The goal is completely open, he's lining it up, he takes the shot -"

There was a brilliant white flash of lightning. The radio went silent. The security monitors shut off, and the lamp on the security guard's desk went black. Bob blinked his eyes in the dark.

His night vision destroyed, he waited, staring into the darkness whilst fumbling for his torch. His hand touched the cold steel of the switch, and he flicked it on. From the stair-well, he saw a steady orange flash, on, off, on, off, and he followed it to investigate. There was a hum, and a click as the emergency electricity kicked in. Gazing around, bull recognised the box of the fire alarm.

A mechanical-sounding voice spoke loudly over the speaker system.

"Warning: There is a fire in the building, please proceed to the nearest fire exit."

I need to ring someone, he thought

He reached into his blazer pocket, pulled out a mobile phone, and punched in the Professor's number.

Rhea answered the phone. "Hello?"

"Hey Rhea, is the Professor there with you? I've got a fire alarm going off down here, what should I do?"

"Head downstairs to the fire point and grab the fire extinguisher and then check the panel to see where the fire is. If you feel you can handle it, then please try to put the fire out. If you can't, then get out of there, and we will deal with it,". There was a scuffling noise as Rhea cupped her hand over the handset, and Bob heard her saying, "Come on Uncle Eric, there's a fire at the Lab,". Bob hung up and put the phone back in his pocket.

The generator whined to a stop.

"Dammit, I knew I should have filled that with more fuel," he said to himself, mumbling in the darkness.

The beam on the torch flashed across the familiar shape of a fire extinguisher. He grabbed it, then ventured downstairs, searching for signs of fire. Looking around each room, all he could find was the usual tech equipment the scientists used to create the unique inventions they were making. There was a weird hovering bicycle, a strange-looking necklace with a teardrop shape, some odd-looking foods, and something that looked like it should be in a spy movie.

———

The last door at the end of the corridor lead to the main lab, and Bob saw a flickering light. Inside the lab, there was a loud humming sound, and he could smell something. *What was that smell? Onions - no, Frying bacon - yes! Why could he smell bacon?*

Bull looked around for the source of the odour, and then came across the body of a naked man, completely motionless, lying on the table. He walked closer to see if the man was okay.

As he approached, the smell of bacon and the odour of blood surrounded him, and the clicking footsteps of his shoes on the hard floor became more of a sticky slapping noise, as he stepped into an unknown substance.

Looking down, he spotted all the goo that the Professor and Rhea had warned him about but quickly put his mind back on track, to see if the man was okay.

His army medical training kicked in, and within seconds he was checking the man's pulse, and performing mouth-to-mouth resuscitation, pumping his hands on his chest, and breathing life-giving air into his lungs. A few moments later, the man's eyes flickered open, and he breathed in sharply. He was alive!

CHAPTER 2

Twenty years earlier
Date: 21 May 2008
Zacs 10th Birthday
Location: Zacs House, Kisterwich

Zac threw the sheets and duvet off the bed in excitement as he woke to the familiar sound of the birthday song being played downstairs. His parents had repeated this ritual now since he was 5 years old.

He hurriedly threw on his school uniform, brushed his hair and teeth, grabbed his schoolbag, and then ran downstairs to share breakfast with the family at the dining table.

"Hey honey, have you seen my mobile phone?" asked his dad.

"Have you lost it again?" his mum called out from the kitchen. "Honestly, I don't know why you got that thing in the first place. It spends more time lost than it does found."

Rebecca and Mike saw Zac and wished him Happy Birthday.

"Double digits now," said his father proudly as he handed the birthday boy a parcel. Zac sat down at the breakfast table and breathed in the awesome smells of sausage, bacon, eggs, and baked beans, overshadowed slightly by the smell of almost-burnt toast, his favourite. He tore open the wrapping paper, and his eyes lit up.

"Thank you, it's just what I wanted," he said with a beaming smile. He admired the book in brown leather, its gold inlay on the title at the front, and breathed in the smell as he thumbed through it, his very own brand-new journal.

"Here you go sweetheart," said his mum passing him another parcel.

"Is this what I think it is?" he asked with wild excitement.

Zac eagerly tore at the paper, and he just looked in amazement.

He looked closely at the present, stroking the varnish on the wooden presentation box.

Easing the box open, his excitement grew and grew.

The handcrafted wooden box contained the best present ever. But this was not just any present. This was the pen that Zac had wanted since last year. This was the RealPen Pro fountain pen, the best fountain pen ever, with a real gold nib. With great satisfaction Zac peeled the cellophane wrapper from the pen, exposing the beautiful deep red lacquered outer shell, with his initials in gold: J.I.D. - James Isaac Drummond.

They all hugged each other.

"This is the best birthday ever!"

Zac looked up as he heard the noticeably heavy footsteps of his brother as he walked down each step.

"Elephant!" shouted Zac to his brother.

As Zac ate his breakfast with his presents by his side, Dylan walked past his little brother's plate, grabbing a sausage.

"Hey, get your own," Zac said.

"Okay, keep your wig on". Dylan gave Zac an envelope. "Swap you," he said.

Zac opened the card, read the cheesy greeting, and pocketed the ten-pound note. "Cheers Bro".

"Shall we go by car today, sweetie?" asked his mum. Zac smiled.

"Yes, please Mum," he said. "That's settled then," she answered.

"Hey, how come he gets a lift to school, and I don't?" Asked Dylan with a disappointed look on his face.

"When it's your birthday, you will get a lift," replied his mother.

"I'm off to Bennys to get a lift then," he replied.

"Bex, could you pick up some milk and bread while you are out?" came his muffled father's voice from the open fridge.

"Already on the list" replied Rebecca making a mental note.

"Go get your shoes on, young man,".

"Okay," and with that, Zac put his knife, fork and plate into the sink and then headed to the shoe rack in the porch. Rebecca spoke to Dylan quietly, and Zac sensed they were talking about his surprise party that his Nana Iris had let slip about a week ago.

Dylan shouted "I'm off to college now, see you later bruv" he closed the door, and before Zac said anything, the letterbox opened, and Dylan shouted "Happy Birthday". Moments later, Zac was putting on his shoes and blazer. He grabbed his bag, opened the door and went out to the car.

The journey to school was great. The sun was shining and Zac had a beaming smile. From the back seat of the car, he could see his mum's reflection in the rear-view mirror. Her blue eyes, long blonde hair in a bun and comforting warm smile made him realise just how happy he was to be alive. This was the best day ever, and nothing could ruin it!

The car pulled up outside the building, and Zac opened the passenger door, grabbing his bag. His mum asked him for a kiss goodbye, but Zac pulled away shyly with a comment about the fact that he was 'too old for all that', and that it was embarrassing.

The Charles Cramer High School was a grand building from the 1930s, adorned with the usual architecture of that era. Big wooden doors, small windows, and a 'this is where you come to learn' look about it. These days, however, there was a school hall with larger windows, and the students experienced a much less strict method of teaching, where the pupils were no longer required to sit in rows, but around tables.

Punishments were no longer dished out, instead, positive methods were used to encourage the students to help them learn. The teachers also had a relaxed, friendly manner and called each other by their first names. Zac loved coming here, it was much better than his old school, he could learn more about reading, writing, maths, and science, and best of all, it had a library. They hugged, and his mum got back in the car. Zac walked into the schoolyard towards a group of friends proudly displaying his '10' badge. They huddled around him to admire it.

CHAPTER 3

Several Hours Later

At Charles Cramer High School, the hand on the classroom clock ticked slowly, too slowly for Zac. Looking at the clock, the second hand just seemed to move in slow-motion, Tick, tiiick, tiiiiiiiiick. This lesson would not end any sooner while he kept looking at it.

Zac was bored. The lesson was boring. School was boring. His teacher was… boring. The boring second hand on the boring clock was going so boringly slooooooow. When would this lesson ever end?

The fuzzy classroom window looking out to the corridor went dark as someone approached class 12.

Zac watched the handle turn, and the door opened. Walking into the room was a man whom Zac had never seen before.

"What can I do for you?" asked Zac's teacher.

He asked to speak to her, and she left Darren Black to look after the class while she went into the corridor to chat with the man.

After a few minutes; at least that's what it felt like to Zac, Ms Northek came back into the classroom and asked Darren to sit back in his seat. She sat down in her chair and stayed silent for a moment, staring out of the window in a daze, collecting her thoughts and deciding how she should deal with the information she had just received. After a moment, she stood up facing the students. "Children, put down your pens and stop what you're doing, Jenny Taylor, you too". Jenny turned around and stared at Ms Northek. "I've just been told that the dining hall is already in use today, so we can all eat our lunch in class. Those of you who have hot lunches, you will eat in here too." The children smiled and chattered to each other. This was a marvellous opportunity to enjoy food in class, an occasion usually saved for special days like the last day of term or non-school uniform days. In excitement, the volume of chatter rose, and Ms Northek clapped her hands to attract their attention. The children quietened and listened to what she had to say. "Lunch time is still the same as normal, 12:15, so you all still have 27 minutes to be getting on with your work."

Zac sighed. *27 boring minutes left*, he thought. Zac, fed up with the lesson, decided he needed to help the time go faster by doing something less boring, and with that, his hand shot into the air. "Excuse me, Miss, may I go to the toilet". She glanced again at her watch and grabbed one of the hall passes on her desk. "Okay Zac, here's a hall pass". He left the classroom with the ticket in his hand, and a smile on his face then walked down the hallway towards the toilets.

———

Reading the graffiti inside the cubicle, Zac smiled at the rude poetry, and the "I was 'ere" comments, finished what he was doing, and then pulled the flush.

He washed his hands and walked up the corridor when he noticed his friend Evan walking towards him.

"Evan" Zac called.

"Happy birthday buddy."

"Thanks mate," he smiled, and then his face dropped.

"Today is sooooooo boring."

"I know right, I asked to go to the toilet just to get out of class."

"No way, me too…."

"Hey, where are the hall monitors?"

They stopped and looked around. The place was quiet, and no one was to be seen.

"Good question. I can't see anyone. Although, I saw something weird a minute ago."

"What?" Evan asked

"A man came to our class, spoke to Ms Northek, and afterwards, she let me go to the toilet with no problems,".

"What? 'No dilly-dallying' or 'straight there and straight back' like usual?"

"Nope,"

"That is weird,"

They chatted for a moment, and as they walked back to their lessons, they walked past the main hall doors.

And just like that, as if the school bell had rung, the classroom doors flung open and students left their classrooms, and all headed the same way, towards the hall.

As children walked straight past the hall doors and headed on down the corridor, curiosity got the better of Evan and Zac, and in the hustle and bustle, and with no one to stop them, the boys investigated what was going on.

Opening the hall door, they looked around in surprise to see rows upon rows of fold-up beds with medical equipment beeping, and bags of solutions hanging from wheeled metal poles. Several doctors were walking around with clipboards, electronic tablets and stethoscopes. Zac scanned the room, as someone approached them.

"Hello, my name is Doctor Rhys Liefe, who are you here to see?".

"Erm, we erm..." started Evan.

"Nit nurse?" said Zac with a cheeky grin, but the doctor didn't seem to be in a joking mood.

A woman in a lab coat with a stethoscope walked over and whispered into the Doctors' ears.

He stood back, picked up a loud hailer, and talked into it.

"Attention everyone," he said as it boomed across the room, grabbing everyone's attention. "We have over a hundred incoming casualties, and some walking wounded coming in, I need everyone to get to their stations, arrivals will begin in the next few minutes."

The boys watched in amazement as people rushed around, and Dr Rhys turned to them and said, "It's time for you to leave. We have planned for you to wait for your parents in classroom 6. Please go there straight away". He pointed down the corridor, and then as the boys headed off, he picked up his electronic tablet and typed into it.

Zac and Evan left the room and walked down the corridor towards classroom 6.

———

When they got there, Zac noticed the tables were no longer out, and classroom chairs were in rows. The TV trolley was at the front of the class.

Children sat in chairs watching Eggy and friends - a cartoon about a superhero egg, and his best friend tomato, who help each other keep their veggie friends safe from the evil cheese monster. The cartoon, although aimed at younger children, was also popular among 10-year-olds.

There was a knock on the door, and a woman wearing a blue smock and white apron asked to speak to the teacher outside the room.

The children laughed as Eggy tipped some custard over the cheese monster, then watched as tomato giggled.

The cheese-monsters cronies came in to fight with Eggy, and then…

The screen showed up bright red with white bold writing "NEWS FLASH!".

The children looked at one another.

"What?" said one child in frustration.

"That's not fair," said another.

"Flick the channel Susie, you're the closest," said someone else.

"Yea Susie, turn over to a different one."

She stood up and pressed the buttons, but it was no use, the news flash was on all of them, so she sat down and watched, and they waited.

"This is Brent Jastock reporting from Channel 14 news, at the Kisterwich dam, where residents have told us they see cracks in the dam wall. Let's go live to Kit Gersairy on the ground."

"Thanks Brent. I'm here with Dan Eiseling, who lives just down the road here in Kisterwich. Dan, can you tell us what you saw?"

"Yes, Kit. Well, my wife and I were sleeping, I sleep like a log, but there was a massive rumble, and it woke both of us up. At first, we thought it was an earthquake, but we don't get earthquakes here, so we quickly dismissed it." He motioned his arms as if shaking from an earthquake.

"My wife Helen looked out of the window, and she just froze, unable to speak. I couldn't see very well, so she passed me the binoculars, and that was when we called the police. They told us to stay in our house, and that rescue would come along soon."

He pointed his arm at the dam wall with water now spewing out of it. The ground rumbled again, and some debris came loose from the wall of the dam. The water turned from a gentle spew to a sudden gush and turned the earth at the bottom of the dam into a mud soup.

Another rumble interrupted them, and the camera switched to the eye in the sky once more.

Stunned, the journalist didn't know what to say as the camera zoomed in on the crack which had started to spider its way further up the wall. The cameraman panned the camera to show the viewers the dam, the crack, the water, the mud soup, the farmland, and then across the entire town.

"Earlier this morning, confusion and bad tempers rose, pushing the situation into something terrifying. An unidentified woman pulled out a firearm and let off a couple of shots, turning the evacuation from an orderly event into one of panic and pandemonium. Armed forces detained the woman, and paramedics have treated two people involved in a fistfight."

The camera in the helicopter panned around, went slightly out of focus, and then zoomed in towards the dam wall. The children could see water coming out of the wall.

"Are you getting this?" Brent asked.

"I sure am" the camera operator confirmed, giving Brent a thumbs up.

"I don't know if you can see this at home folks, but I am looking at substantial damage, and water is flooding out from the cracks in the dam."

The sound of army helicopters drowned out the news reporter's voice, and the camera followed them as they flew overhead.

The camera swung round from the dam, and the television showed the helicopters hovering, with the soldiers expertly sliding down the ropes, landing on the tarmac of the supermarket car park.

"We now go live to Kit Gersairy on the ground for more information,".

The camera switched from the eye in the sky to the ground crew, and there was a pretty blonde woman with a channel 14 microphone in her hand to the right of the camera.

She stood close to the dam, enough not to be in imminent danger, but also to get the entire wall into the shot.

"Kit Gersairy here, reporting for Channel 14 news at the Kisterwich dam." She began.

"The dam has been here for well over one hundred and twenty-five years, and last month Channel 14 visited to share the town's anniversary of the dam. Now, those cheerful faces of celebration are turning to those of fear and dread as they struggle to come to terms with what is happening with the dam walls. The army has arrived, to coordinate a full-scale evacuation of the entire town. As you can see behind me, the walls have sustained significant damage, and it is not clear if this is a terrorist attack or just a freak accident."

The ground crew camera panned from the reporter to some coaches driving down the street, and then to the bottom of the ropes where the soldiers had started to gather.

The men quickly stood in line, and another guy in front shouted something indistinct, then pointed in a few different directions, and the men followed their orders, peeling into different directions, and knocking on doors to help start the evacuation.

———

The Channel 14 Helicopter hovered above Kisterwich police station. Brent swept his hand through his hair to make it look tidy, but the wind outside wasn't doing him any favours. He adjusted his glasses. The cameraman focussed his lens and activated the light and camera.

"Welcome back to Channel 14 News. I am Brent Jastock, and this is a news update on the Heyworth Dam in Kisterwich."

The picture of Brent miniaturised into a small overlay in the top right corner of the screen. The rest of the screen showed a live feed from the helicopter, with a bird's-eye view of some coaches driving through the town to collect a group of waiting evacuees.

"As you can see, the Army has got this evacuation under-way, and these coaches will help to take the citizens of Kister-wich up to safety, so they can drain the reservoir, and fix the damage to the dam wall."

The coaches bore left down the main street, pulled into the car park, and stopped. People started pushing and shoving to get on the coach, and a soldier picked up a loud hailer and started talking into it.

The group of townsfolk formed an orderly queue and then filled the coach. A second coach pulled up behind the first. More people arrived, and they and the rest of the queue turned from an orderly evacuation into a mass frenzy, running, almost mob-like towards the coaches, each person in a race to be the first to get a seat to safety, as another rumble came from the dam wall.

Zac's eyes were fixed on the television. He tried to pick out his mother, father and brother from all the other pixels on the screen.

The camera zoomed out, Brent's overlay picture disap-peared, and the screen was a mass of hundreds of pixels all fighting to get onto the coach.

Zac squinted, he thought he saw his brother, then lost him among the crowd. The man that Zac was watching turned towards the camera, and Zac, realising it wasn't Dylan, started scanning the rest of the screen to find them.

Hundreds more people leaving their houses grouped up into the car park, and more coaches followed.

"They just need to get on the bus," said one child.

"And stop shoving," said another.

The noise of the second crowd was almost deafening, people on the television started crying, and shouting, and there were arguments and frayed tempers. Someone needed to get this situation in order. It was almost as if people on the television could hear what the children were thinking when suddenly, a shot rang out.

The Camera zoomed in to show a soldier with his rifle in the air, then slowly lowering the weapon, aiming it at the crowd.

The crowd went silent, and no one moved.

The soldier shouted something, and people split up into groups. The women and children went onto the coaches first, followed by the men, and the second and third coaches were on their way, following the same route out of town, and heading up the hill towards Newhaven.

One child stuck his hand out and shouted, "That's my mum!". A girl spotted her Gran.

All the children sat up and look closely at the screen to see if they could see family members or people they recognised.

The picture on the TV switched to a split screen with Brent and Kit. The Children watched as Brent and Kit discussed how well the evacuation was going, given the urgency, and that they had both seen nothing on a scale like it in their entire careers. While it was exciting, and scary for them, it all became rather boring for Zac and the other children. Kit and Brent chatted about the history of the dam, Zac had already been on the walks around the lake, and he knew all there was for a ten-year-old to know.

There was a massive rumble on the TV, and both newscasters fell silent.

The camera instantly swung to the dam, and the images of Brent and Kit faded from the screen. The crack in the wall turned into a split from the middle, expanding outwards like a spider's web.

The helicopter manoeuvred to another position, and the camera panned from the dam towards the coaches. The children cheered as the coaches got to the top of the hill.

The next few moments seemed like one of those horror movies, an end-of-the-world scene, as the wall disintegrated, and the water just left the lake, in the same way, that a mug of tea loses all its water when it's dropped onto the floor, in a slow-motion moment.

Within seconds the camera wobbled as the shock wave buffeted the helicopter, and at that moment they could hear Kit calling out, "God help us, please help us," from below.

The children watched as the water hit the houses, carrying on with its reign of destruction, house after house, street after street, each street engulfed in water in seconds.

There was a painfully loud hiss of static on the microphone, and Brent sat there in the helicopter, totally speechless as Kits' communication ended.

Millions and millions of gallons of water broke loose from the confines of the dam, and thundered through the town, nature's unimaginable force, in an unending torrent.

The camera feed cut off, and the picture on the screen showed the channel was experiencing technical difficulties.

Although several miles away, the school and surrounding area felt vibrations as the water emptied from the dam and flooded the town. The noise was terrifying over the TV. Within moments the ground started shaking at the school, the TV set wobbled, children's chairs and tables shook, and the windows rattled. The classroom clock fell off, and onto the floor with a resounding crash.

The children cried. They had seen the first two coaches come up the hill, but what had happened to the other 3 coaches?

The door flew open, startling the children, and Nurse Oshwen looked at the children. Some were crying, and some were in shock. Zac had tears running down his face.

She looked at the television and switched it off.

Another doctor entered.

"Nurse Tanya Oshwen, can you step outside for a moment, please?"

She followed the doctor, and after a moment, the door opened again.

"Zac, your mum is here, and she would like to see you,".

Zac's heart leapt. She was alive.

He hugged the nurse, and they went to find his mum.

Zac looked in amazement at the hall. He had never seen the hall this busy, not even on a parent/teacher evening, no one had.

Across the sea of people, he scanned through the hustle and bustle, and then his eyes met with his mother's.

The bustling sounds changed to a background mumble, as the surrounding people became a blur, and all he could focus on was his mum.

His eyes scanned the room for a route, and he let go of Nurse Tanya's hand, quickly pushing through the crowds of people, and bumping into Mr Northek on the way.

Throwing his arms around his mum, they wept uncontrollably, and just stayed there for what seemed like about five minutes.

As Zac and his mum hugged a long, motionless hug, his mum whispered into his ear.

"I love you, Zac,".

"I love you too, mum."

They hugged.

Moments later, Dylan joined them.

"Where's Dad?" Dylan asked.

"He's on another bus, I saw him on the front of the bus behind mine."

The conversation stopped.

Time ticked by slowly, but their father still didn't arrive. It had been several hours since the first and second coaches had dropped everyone off, and the darkness was making it harder for volunteers and rescue services to go out, and look for buses three, four, and five, until tomorrow at least.

CHAPTER 4

6 Months Later
    3rd November 2008
    The lady Mayor and the vicar stood on either side of something tall, covered in burgundy velvet fabric, edged with golden trim and tassels. Whatever it was, it had a granite plinth. In front of them was a large crowd, gathered on top of Appleton Hill, overlooking what was left of the town of Kisterwich.

Most people were wearing black, with their heads bowed low. "We are gathered here to remember those who died in the flood, and to erect this monument as an everlasting reminder that we will never forget," said the mayor. The vicar read some passages from his bible, and as the gentle wind blew from behind him, tussling the tufts of grey hair over his ears, it carried his words over the entire crowd listening in silence.

They all prayed, and a few of the townsfolk stood up to call out the names of loved ones they had lost. It wasn't long before Zac's father's name was read out, and from then on, he heard very little, and just felt his mum's reassuring hug as she stood next to him.

His gaze carried on past the vicar, and over the town. It looked like a building graveyard with brick, metal and concrete corpses stripped of any identifying features, weathered like sandcastles in the wind, indistinguishable from one another. Pylons and streetlights looked like twisted towers of metal, bringing with them electrical hazards and power cuts that had plunged the town into complete darkness. Tidemarks on the sides of the buildings showed where floodwater once was, and the place his family had originally called home was nothing now but a ghost town full of scattered remains, with only the cinema, the bank, Glenbrook Abbey and the old well still in good standing. Despite the efforts of the Army and the emergency services, no one had a chance, and all rescue missions had long since been abandoned after everyone had cleared out. The military had moved in and erected an electrified perimeter fence with razor-wire encircling the town. Warning signs on the chain-link fences "Keep out - Trespassers will be shot - By Order of the Army and Danger: High Voltage - 10,000v". At the entrance to the town was a rising roadblock buried into the road with hazard warning signs painted on it, and an armed guard sat in a small hut wearing camouflaged clothing with an SA-80 standard-issue assault rifle by his side. The sign next to the hut read Military Station: C472 - Kisterwich. Throughout most of the town, the streets and pavements, which once bustled with traffic and pedestrians, were now littered with rubble and debris from the knee-high remnants of buildings, completely levelled during the disaster.

The boy's attention shifted as the Lady Mayor of Newhaven stood in front of the microphone. She made a small speech, tugged on a gold cord and the burgundy velvet cover slid off revealing a large granite cross, ten feet tall. At the base was a representation of the dam with a large, engraved plaque. Zac scanned his eyes across the plaque, and although the words were too small to see, where he was standing, he could make out rows upon rows of names etched into the metal. The lines on the plaque became blurry and his mind filled with memories. He remembered watching tv with his father, and the way his dad would shout at the commentators, that he could be a better referee. Memories flooded back of that day at the lake when his brother was trying to get in the boat, did the splits and fell in. Memories of the way his mum's hair used to blow around in the wind, and the smiles that his mum and dad always gave each other made his lips curl upward, and for a moment he forgot where he was. They were so in love, and it showed. Not that 'gross love', where they were always kissing and embarrassing him and his brother, but that 'holding hands and cuddling' love, where they could watch a film with each other and drink the odd glass of wine now and then. A million more memories exploded in his brain all at once, and then, as soon as they appeared, they had gone again. He let go of his mums' hand, loosened his tie, unbuttoned his shirt collar, and a tear ran down his face. And like that, the service ended. People started to leave in silence.

In the distance, a car disrupted the sombreness with its screeching sirens and flashing lights, and some of the mourners turned to see what was going on. The noise got louder, and the car stopped just metres away from the crowd. Two burly-looking men got out, and they marched towards the mourners.

"Excuse us, ladies and gentlemen, we just need to talk to someone," said the smaller cop.

"What's this all about officer?" asked the mayor.

The second cop stepped forward, opened his jacket, pulled some papers out of his pocket, unfolded them, and then thrust his arm outstretched towards the crowd, with the papers crumpled in his fist.

"Rebecca Drummond of 19 Ashbock Road, Kisterwich, we

have a warrant for your arrest, in connection to the bombing of the Heyworth Dam." the second cop said out loud.

The crowd gasped, and everyone looked at Zac's mum.

"What? That's impossible!" she exclaimed, with a look of complete disbelief on her face.

"We have evidence, you're coming with us."

The tallest officer placed his handcuffs around Rebecca's wrists as the crowd watched in shock.

"She blew up the dam?" asked one man.

"I knew it was her, I never liked her," said another.

"My husband died, because of you!" an angry crowd member shouted.

Dylan looked at the floor, not sure what to say or do.

"It wasn't…"

Zac cut Rebecca off. "Mum, I can't believe this, Dad is gone because of you!". He reached into his pocket, pulled out the RealPen Pro, tossed it on the floor, and then in a deliberate moment of anger, he stamped on it, smashing it to pieces.

Rebecca looked at him. What had she done? Why couldn't she remember?

"I HATE YOU" cried Zac, and he turned to his grandmother, and hugged her, sobbing, as his mother was put into the car, and driven away. Dylan just watched.

It couldn't be her, he thought to himself.

CHAPTER 5

3 0 years later
        21 May 2038
        Zacs 40th Birthday

Angelic shafts of light shone across the ocean, over the tops of the distant mountains, through valleys, and fields and down into the town of Newhaven, as the sun burst through the horizon, lighting up the rooftops of the buildings, trees, and roads.

At the top of Appleton hill in Ye olde Appletree farm, a rooster stood up tall, flapped its wings, stretched its neck, then pushed out his chest, and let out a deafening 'cock-a-doodle-doo' breaking the silence across the sleepy town.

The meteodrone flew around in its daily routine, checking for road congestion, traffic accidents, weather, temperature, and barometric readings, and taking scenic photographs and other data for the early morning news report.

As it buzzed through the sky, the camera on the meteodrone looked upon the solar-panelled houses, took a sunlit photograph of the "Welcome to Newhaven" sign with its "Winner of Green Scene of the year" award, then panned around to include the mist on the sea in the distance.

The town was serene, for the moment. It would soon be bustling with people. With its natural beauty and stance on recycling, solar power, and clean emissions, Newhaven had become a great place to live.

Inside his apartment, Zac's eyes flickered open, and he looked around in the dimness of his bedroom.

"Holovision on" he called out. At the end of his bed, a shiny black bar four feet long, two inches wide, and an inch high activated. It emitted two beams of light from the top of the bar at each end. Each beam lit up at 45-degree angles, shining a beam of light towards the centre of the holobar. When they met in the middle, they created a 3D holographic image. The holographic ray was showing a 3D music video from the 20's band "Curves of Verox" with their chart-topping rendition of "Even hate needs love".

"Volume up" Zac instructed the holobar. As it got louder, he sat himself up in bed for a few minutes gazing at the reruns, yawning and stretching.

An alarm buzzed from somewhere in the flat, the lights in his bedroom illuminated slowly to 50% and Zac got out of bed.

He walked into the bathroom and stood in front of the mirror.

As the lights got slowly brighter, Zac stared at his reflection.

The facial detection in the mirror's camera scanned the bleary-eyed man and stopped the alarm. A voice from the mirror spoke, "Good morning Mr Drummond, and Happy 40th Birthday." A picture of a simple-looking cupcake with a candle on it appeared on the screen and the birthday song played. "Blow out the candles and make a wish," said the animated mirror.

He paused for a moment, pulled a "go away" face, then flicked his hand away from him towards the mirror as if shooing a fly, waving the virtual cake away. The cake and the birthday message slid off the screen. "Here is today's outlook," the mirror announced, speaking in a female English accent. His ex-girlfriend never liked it, but he didn't care.

He swept his fingers through his bed hair, styling it as his fingers slid through, and tried to stare, focussing on his hazel eyes at the 40-year-old man looking back at him. His eyes blurred at the mirror, but he could still see the well-trimmed black goatee. He blinked twice, and his autofocus contact lenses switched on, displaying the Luminettes logo briefly, and adjusted themselves until he could see clearly. The enhancements in the new improved back-lit eyewear helped his night vision, very useful considering the lights were only at 50%, but even better when they auto-adjusted to the lower light.

The mirror downloaded the information from the meteo-drone and lit up with icons of the sun and clouds, temperature and weather forecast for the day in the top right-hand corner. It then covered the rest of the mirror with a virtual calendar, and the voice announced today's schedule whilst displaying it on the screen.

He looked for a second, then shooed the calendar away once more and proceeded with his early morning ritual. Sliding out his ultrasonic toothbrush and inserting it into his mouth, he laid the sonobrush onto his tongue. It was a weird-looking lolly stick type thing with no bristles, With the handle of his sonobrush laying on his bottom lip, he gave the handle a gentle squeeze with his upper lip, to jump it into action. Zac clicked the news icon on the mirror and waved the screen in a swiping motion to flick through the articles and the weather reports. The screen mimicked a book, and each swipe showed him the next article.

A beeper on the sonobrush told him that his teeth were now clean, and he poured himself a glass of water, gargling to get rid of the sonic debris, then sprayed his mouth with some mintyfresh. The sonobrush went back into the charging pot and a beep confirmed it was cleaning while the ultraviolet light sanitised it.

Back in the bedroom, he got himself dressed.

He slid his arms into his favourite black shirt with white flecks and pressed the magnetic fasteners until they snapped firmly in place.

Next, he took his wrist phone off the bedside table and draped it onto his wrist, snapping the magnetic clasp together. Aesthetically it wasn't much to look at, just a black circle with a strap, which showed the time when you tapped it, but technologically it was a magnificent work of bio-electronic micro-engineering. Powered by body warmth, it contained some hidden extras.

Inside its sleek black non-important-looking circular frame, the black disc had a Wi-Fi phone inside it. The user would activate the phone by tapping the watch face and talking to it, instructing who to call, adding a contact number and name or asking for directions, and the built-in microphone would take the instructions and complete the desired task. Instead of using a speaker that others could listen in to, the underneath of the wrist phone's black dial would vibrate instead. It would then send these vibrations from the wearer's wrist, across the hand and up to the tip of the finger using bone conduction.

To listen to the call, the wearer would put the forefinger of the user's hand into their ear or touch their finger or hand anywhere onto their face, and it would convert the vibrations to speech that only the wearer could hear. No one could overhear it, because there was no speaker, the ultimate in privacy. The built-in microphone would then allow the caller to hear you.

He eased himself into his black trousers with silver stripes down the seams and slid on his smart black bioplastic shoes, snapping the magnets together in the middle.

Zac called out. "Privacy mode off", and the windows in the apartment unfrosted.

The artificial lighting switched off as the room lit up with the sun's brightness.

To say it lit up with the actual sun was not quite accurate, since the window was not a real window, but a large digital screen embedded in the wall to give the illusion of a window. The image itself was a live feed from the cameras on the outside of the building helping give the illusion that the tenant at Flat 142, 5e Panada Drive, Newhaven was looking outside the window, and not just at the brick wall of the next-door neighbour's flat. This enhanced people's moods and helped the tenants live in cramped spaces that wouldn't have previously been possible. Digital well-being, they called it.

Finally, he grabbed his ID-Fob pendant from the bedside table, gently placed the neck cord over his head, and hung the pendant underneath his shirt, out of sight, and with a small split-second buzz it started up into life, powered from the warmth of his chest. He triple-clicked the centre button of the ID-Fob, and a small vibration alerted Zac to the display on his luminettes, which told him that an autocab was on its way.

Walking into the kitchen Zac glanced at the time on the front of the microwave display - *6:45 am, time to go to work,* he said to himself. Grabbing a berry-pop bar from the basket in the fridge, he then made his way out of his apartment and down the stairs towards the street.

On his way down, Zac's wrist vibrated, and a text flashed up on his luminettes to tell him that the autocab was only one minute away. The street was quiet, apart from the buzz of the meteodrone. As he waited, the brightness of the sun made the Luminette contact lenses go dark, and the warmth was gentle on his hands and face. Getting into the autocab, he called out his intended destination.

"Libros Antiques, Abbernard Lane," he said to the driverless cab. "Certainly Sir" came the robotic reply of the vehicle, and it moved forwards down the street and turned left.

A few moments later, Zac arrived at his destination, and the vehicle stopped. "You have arrived. Autocabs has taken 17 ebits as payment. Thank you for using Autocabs. Have a nice day" Zac got out of the car and walked towards the shop door where his brother was waiting for him.

"Hey Dylan, what brings you here?" Asked Zac with a surprised look on his face.

"You didn't think I would forget my little brother's birthday, do you?" Dylan replied, "I know you don't celebrate it, but I got something special for you. A table at Luigi's."

A ping on a bell made them both look around.

"Hey, Charlie". Zac looked at the postman on his new Velo bike.

"Good morning, Mr Drummond" replied the postal worker with a big smile. He took out a large parcel from his postal bag, then pulled out a small rectangular palm-sized box, with an ID Fob-shaped marking on it, and passed it to Zac.

"Please sign here," said the postman passing the box to the store owner. Zac pressed his ID Fob against it and thumbed the fingerprint reader to confirm the action. The electronic screen on the box lit up and then beeped to show that it confirmed the digital signature, and a confirmation text buzzed on Zac's wristphone, showing up as a notification envelope in the top left corner of his luminettes. Charlie said goodbye, then got on his electro scooter and scooted off down the road to deliver more parcels.

"I've got to go," said Dylan checking his watch while jogging on the spot.

"Will you be helping me at the shop today?"

"Nah, I have to do some research for those books you want, and I need to get home and use my new computer, instead of that crappy thing you've got,"

"It's not crappy, it's a classic," said Zac proudly.

Dylan smirked "See you tomorrow at 7 pm at Luigi's."

"Yep, it's the best place in town," Dylan smiled.

"Haha, it's the only place in town".

Dylan jogged up the road.

Zac fumbled with the ID Fob, unlocking the door.

He brushed against it and some paint flaked off, reminding him that the job needed to be done months ago.

Determined to do something about it this week, to keep his mind off his birthday and the terrible memories it held, he had a good look around the shop front, studying it carefully.

To give Libros Antiques a more authentic look and feel, the outside of the shop had been painted with a white under-coat, on top of the bioplastic window frames. On top of the white undercoat was dark brown paint, textured to look like wood. Now scuffed and worn after years of neglect, some of the undercoats had started to show.

Old Man Frade had painted the windowpanes with a yellow tint to protect the books that originally stood in the window from the harmful rays of the sun. To secure the precious stock from smash-and-grab crimes, and lower the insurance policy, Zac had recently removed the books from the windows and replaced them with LCD panels showing virtual bookshelves which included the shop's books.

This meant he could update the display much faster by adding new books to the computer.

Stuck to the inside of one of the windowpanes was a small sticker with "PHPC certified. The owner of this establishment is a member of the Paperback and Hardback Protection Commission," emblazoned onto it.

In a world where trees are now a protected species, and paper is only allowed to be sold under license, Zac's shop was one of the few places left to hold books.

The front door to the shop was also in the same style as the wood-look window frames, but instead of windowpanes, it had faux wooden panels. Its fake-looking letterbox was pointless since the postal system had been shut down years ago. The only difference was that the brass disc shape, trying to mimic a 5-lever key lock, had no key. Instead, there was a contactless locking system activated by the fingerprint reader and ID-Fob.

Standing outside the shop, Zac held his ID-Fob against the fake-looking antique door lock, pressing his thumb into the fingerprint reader.

A satisfying unlocking clunk of big heavy doors made it obvious that the doors were now open, and he smiled remembering that the custom unlocking sound heavydoor3.mp3 was now one of his main satisfying reasons for getting up and going to work in the morning.

The door creaked open. The creaking sound and the books were the only authentic things in the shop, and while most shop owners would have dealt with the irritating noise, Zac had decided not to bother as he felt it added character.

The inside of the shop was a simple square shape, with bookshelves from floor to ceiling, filled with paperbacks, hardbacks of different sizes, shapes and colours, and a shop counter with more fake-wood panelling. On the counter was a fake-looking phone, an old-fashioned answer machine and a till which also hid an ID Fob reader for book purchases.

He laid the packages on the counter, and looked at his collection of books, regarding them with pride, he was a part of something special, a heritage, and a part of that heritage was to ensure that the books are treated right in the future with any prospective buyers, but also remembering that life wasn't free and that he needed the money too. Sometimes books were scarce. The outstanding books were exceptionally rare and worth a lot of money. Some books were legendary, and you could retire if you sold them for the right price.

Since the trees protection laws over 15 years ago, first editions could no longer be sold, by law. Instead, they were kept in museums or archived in vaults for security. His shop had almost the same worth and value as the big jewellery shops, certainly in value. Zac's shop was one of the top-grossing places in the town, and he did well from it, from time to time. This week, however, was not one of those times.

"Answer machine..." he called out. Nothing happened.

He tried again, and this time the machine lit up, as it waited for the next command.

"Play messages". Again, nothing happened.

"Please play the new messages" he shouted from across the shop floor in a slow deliberate sentence to make sure that the machine heard him properly.

"You have 2 new messages" replied the machine in a robotic voice.

"Would you like to play them?" it asked.

"Yes... please... play... them" Zac replied, rolling his eyes in frustration as he often did when he had to repeat commands to the archaic machine.

From the top of the machine, a square of light projected onto the wall behind the counter.

Immediately some music played, and a man dressed in shirt, tie, and shorts showed off the very latest in fashion for men... the Manklet, a wearable ankle device for men, that not only looks good but also measures your steps, heart rate, oxygen stats, body temperature and much more. Within seconds of the Manklet advert playing, Zac called out "Next... message... please".

Instantly, the machine obliged. Muttering to himself about the machine's inability to block adverts, he watched the next message display in front of him.

This time the machine projected an image of a woman against the shop wall. She was wearing a crisp white blouse, and a light grey suit with the familiar PHPC logo emblazoned on the left pocket. In front of her, she held a shiny metal tube vertically in one hand. The tube was approximately one centimetre wide and 30 centimetres long. Projecting from the middle of the tube was a translucent shimmering page, from which she read.

"This message is for Zac Drummond of Libros Antiques. If you are the account holder, please authenticate with your ID-Fob to continue with the rest of this message." The hologram paused, and Zac held his ID-Fob next to the machine. Instantly the hologram resumed playback of the recorded message.

"Authentication complete. My name is Agent Tammi Santelle and I am from the Paperbacks and Hardbacks Protection Commission." She looked down at the projected rod screen and read. "Your PHPC license is up for renewal in 14 days. To carry on trading in paper antiquities, we require a payment of 1,350 ebits to be available in full by the end of this month. If you cannot pay this amount, we will have no option but to fine you 50,000 ebits, your inventory will be confiscated, and we will revoke your license until you pay the rest of the outstanding balance. If the full amount, including the fine, is not paid within a period of a further ninety days, we will retrieve the funds from the sale of your stock. You can also apply for a lifetime license for a one-time payment of twenty thousand ebits. Please contact us to arrange immediate payment, our number is…"

As the message continued, the words that Agent Santelle said, sounded quieter, and even become a sort of low mumble, slowly turning into unrecognisable background sounds as Zac gazed into the blur of books on the shop walls and tried to work out how he could afford the rest of this months license.

Work had not always been slow, but the nature of his work meant that he spent 80% of his time searching for books and the rest of the time selling them, and because of the rarity of the books each one was priced at an amount which meant a few sales being able to cover the whole PHPC license and then a few more to make a profit. Selling expensive books was difficult, no one came to this side of town anymore, and advertising didn't seem to work for him as well as it could.

Rent wasn't a problem since the shop had been left to him in the original owner's will, his old boss and only real friend as a teenager 'old Jim Frade' who had taught Zac the business from the ground up, ever since his first visit to the shop. They got on so well, Zac often thought of him as the father he no longer had.

That first visit to the shop, he remembered well. It was a warm sunny day, and Zac had come to Newhaven with his mother and brother and had spent most of the day touring the area, the electric buses that drove on the road, how old-fashioned! He remembered the smell of the traffic, that old familiar smell of rubber and warm electric motors.

That time of the surprise picnic in the park where his mother had laid a blanket on the grass. He remembered the picnic hamper and the flavour of the smoked ham and mayonnaise sandwiches, with watermelon for afters, and he remembered his dad was not there. At that point, Zac had reached his teenage years, and childish things seemed so far away now. He wanted to do something meaningful in his life, and from the moment he walked into Mr Frades' shop and saw the books, and breathed in that old paper smell, he was hooked.

————

The aroma of fresh coffee filled Zac's nostrils, drawing him back to real life. He placed the parcels on the counter, walked over to the coffeepot and poured himself a cup.

Zac had only just picked up his coffee cup when the shop bell rang, and a woman entered the shop.

She was a young woman, rather well-to-do, and out of fashion for this side of town, wearing expensive clothes. As she walked around the shop, perusing the titles on the shelves, her perfume filled Zac's nostrils.

"Excuse me," she said in a quiet voice. "I noticed in the window that you have bedsprings, summer, autumn and winter, yet I don't see it on the shelf."

"That sort of literature isn't usually put on the general displays. Let me just grab that for you". He tapped into the computer and looked up the code of the book. After a few moments in the back room, he returned to the shop floor. The woman was holding the parcels he had just been delivered.

"Are these for sale"? She asked looking at the packages.

"I have to catalogue them first. They will be available from this afternoon onwards". Replied Zac with a smile.

The woman put the books back onto the counter, and Zac placed the book from the back room onto a burgundy velvet mat.

Carefully, and with gloved hands, Zac opened the book's protective bioplastic jacket. She marvelled at the quality of the pages.

Next, she inspected the book and asked it to be gift-wrapped.

"Sorry, I've run out, I'll be back in just one moment." He put the book behind the till, then went into the back, coming out a moment later with a roll of wrapping. He wrapped the book, she paid for it and then left.

The parcels weren't much to look at, one was a large rectangular parcel wrapped in see-through bioplastic acrylic. Zac could see a small stack of books and a letter, and another wrapped in plain brown paper with the words "Mr Z Drummond" written on the front, in a computer-typed label.

The first parcel was obvious, looking at the three books inside, he smiled at the copy of "The sweet and savoury recipe book of yesteryear", flipped it over and behind it spotted the "History of the frozen wasteland" a book about the Arctic, and that copy of "Blake Gladwell – Bionic Detective, Episode 4" which he slid into a protective clear bioplastic jacket and added to the growing collection of Blake Gladwell books already on the shelf.

Next, he drew his attention to the last book. Plain brown paper was unusual to see these days, very expensive, and incredibly rare. The events of that morning had happened so quickly, that he couldn't even remember signing for it. Examining it, he looked for a postmark, or sender's address, and was surprised to find it didn't have either.

On the front of the packet, there were two words. *For Zac.*

Inside the parcel was a small book leather bound approximately 4 inches wide, 6 inches tall, and about 1 inch thick, which still looked as new as it had on his 10th birthday when his father had given it to him. On the front was just one word in the centre of an embossed gold frame.

JOURNAL

The only thing written inside the diary was his name. He remembered wanting so much to treat is as his best friend, and fill it with various writings, feelings, poetry, texts, and important things to write about, but now all he wanted to do was write sad things about how he was missing his father, and how angry he was at his mother. The last time he had seen this book, was at school on that horrible day, and he had always wondered what happened to it. This was one book he would never want to lose again.

He packed it up and put it in his pocket.

After he had finished cataloguing the books, Zac put them into protective bioplastic jackets, marked their prices and arranged them in the VacuFlow sterilised vacuum fridge.

He poured himself another coffee, and the familiar sound of the shop-door bell tinkled as a man who Zac recognised as a collector, entered the shop.

They chatted for a while, and the man bought three books, made a few enquiries and then left.

By the end of the day he had sold several books,

amounting to a generous turnover. Zac was happy that he could afford this month's bills, and even though he was still struggling with the payment for the PHPC license fee, he decided to close the shop earlier than usual.

He locked the door and took his journal with him, knowing it would be safer back at his apartment. The weather was pleasant, so he walked, taking in the evening air and enjoying the feeling of a good day's work done.

Not much happened on the way home, in fact, not that he could remember, because the journey seemed to go so fast. He was too busy thinking about the journal and everything it contained, its history, the note from his mum, and the book it came in. And then he remembered it was his birthday, the fun times he used to have with his parents, and the smiles turn to sadness as he remembered the tragedy of the Heyworth Dam and the "big flood".

The next moment he knew, he was closing the front door of his apartment building.

CHAPTER 6

The movement-activated light brightened up the hallway as Zac walked towards his apartment. He walked in, then kicked the door closed with the heel of his foot, as he headed towards the living room.

"Holovision on". The 3d image appeared in front of Zac, and the weather was the first thing he saw.

Zac poured himself a whiskey and fell asleep on the settee watching reruns of "The Last Laugh" comedy show.

Within moments, he was back at home, in Kisterwich, his mum was making breakfast, his father was struggling to put a tie on, and his brother came up behind Zac and ruffled his little brothers' hair, and then stole a sausage from his plate. It was a normal day, just like every day.

The radio was playing happy birthday. He finished his breakfast, went to put his pot in the sink, and ran the water to rinse out the bowl. After the bowl was clean, he turned the tap to switch off the water, but the water didn't stop, instead, it slowed down to a trickle, then a slow-motion drip. The voices of his family had turned from the breakfast conversation to slow-motion murmurs, at almost a quarter of the speed that he was used to hearing. That drip... he watched it patiently, deliberately, willing it to stop.

It got larger and larger, getting heavy enough to fall off the lip of the tap, and the surrounding sounds, the chatter of a morning breakfast, the clanking of cutlery against crockery as the food was being eaten, slowed down to a low, deep lull.

The drop, heavy now, fell with a resounding splash that broke the silence, and another formed. Another drop, faster and larger than the first one, except it didn't fall. It just kept increasing, getting fuller and fuller. Within seconds the drip was no longer recognisable and was the size of an enormous balloon. Zac watched in disbelief. This wasn't possible. Then the weirdest thing happened. The balloon water bubble exploded, covering Zac, and the tap gushed water at high speed and sprayed everywhere. Panicking, he tried to turn the tap off, but the water stream just got stronger.

Just when he thought it couldn't get any more dangerous, the metal tap rose high above the sink, pulling the fixings off the sink, and taking copper tubing with it. The copper tubing got longer and longer, and the tap on the end reached the kitchen ceiling. As the ceiling and tap touched each other, the copper tubing instantly changed to a flexible hose, and twisted and turned with the pressure, spraying jets of water all over the kitchen, whipping the hose about uncontrollably. Zac turned around to look at his family for help, but they were just sitting at the table, eating their breakfast, completely oblivious to what was going on.

His legs felt something wet. Looking down, he saw the water had reached his waist.

A gentle breeze blew across his face and he looked up to see that the walls of the house were pulled apart as if ripped by the force of a hurricane, but there was no sign of wind, no swaying trees, no ripples in the water, just a gentle breeze on his face. The water filled up the outside of the house, the street, and the neighbourhood with frightening speed. With ferocity and force, the walls were torn apart, and the water took the tiled wall, sink, and cupboards. His mum, dad, and brother, still sat at the breakfast table, floated off down the street, completely unaware of what was going on,

Zac tried to call out to his family, but the sound of the water drowned out his cries, and they were too far away to hear. It wasn't long before they were all out of sight, and all he could hear was the water and a faint beeping noise.

Wading through the water in the direction that the living room had gone, desperately trying to find his family, he slipped on something and fell flat on his face on a settee, which looked just like the one in his flat, banging his head on the arm.

His head pounding, the beeping got louder. He looked around and watched as the house around him, and all the water just vanished. Everything went white.

Zac woke up.

CHAPTER 7

Still, half-dazed by the strange dream, he looked around him. He had flung his duvet across the room and spilt the whiskey he had all over his legs (which explained the wet part of his dream). The beeping continued.

His eyes tried to adjust, but couldn't. The only light available was the buildings' black lights, and the glow from the corner of his eye, instantly recognisable, as the fire alarm exit arrow.

Fire alarm, that's what the beeping is, thought Zac as he quickly got up off the sofa, rubbing his elbow.

The emergency lighting had flooded the room with black light, and as Zac looked around bleary-eyed, he made out the special ultraviolet-painted arrows that glowed with the black light to prepare for such an event. He got up and followed the glowing arrows on the floor to the front door of his apartment and down the stairs towards the fire door.

Outside were several disgruntled people all standing by the designated fire point, one wearing a dressing gown, another man was bare-chested, wearing only a pair of jeans. The woman and her child who lived next door to Zac were there too, along with many others. The caretaker was looking at a tablet and counting the heads of everyone assembled.

After approximately 20 minutes, the fire crew arrived, and the chief confirmed yet another failure by the dodgy fire alarm system as the grumpy tenants went back inside, while one or two stayed and had stern words with the caretaker.

Zac climbed the stairs, the black light still illuminating the safety paint arrows and went inside his apartment.

Flopping onto his bed and kicking his shoes off, he rolled over to go back to sleep when something caught his eye.... A glow of writing... on the front of his journal.

He could hardly believe his eyes, and as he picked up the book, he stared at it, his luminettes trying to focus in the darkness. It was then that he read the words. *Property of Professor Eric Mullins.*

Intrigued by his discovery, he opened the cover and looked inside. The pages of the book were full of glowing orange drawings, lots of schematics and technical stuff, diary entries, and more.

He read, excited and enthused with what he had found. Zac scanned through the book for a moment, then read from page 1.

He checked the time and yawned. 4:03 am.

After a while, his eyes drifted, and the words started to merge into each other,

The more he tried to read, the heavier his eyelids became, until he succumbed to the land of zzz. His eyelids closed all the way, and he drifted off to sleep again.

———

The pattering of the rain coming from the speakers on the fake windows woke Zac up. He stirred and remembered the events of the previous evening.

The delivery, the woman, the book, the eerie glowing writing... *the book! Where was the book?*

He fumbled around the side of his bed, and found it on the floor, wedged between the bed and the table. Picking it up, he noticed the eerie glowing writing wasn't there, and as he thumbed through the book itself, all he saw were the journal entries from when he was younger. Annoyed at himself that he had probably been dreaming again, he put the book down on the bed, went to the kitchen and made himself a cup of coffee.

Yawning, he walked through to the spare bedroom office, poured a slug of whiskey into his coffee and set his mug down on the desk.

The office was a pretty simple place, a chair to sit on next to a desk with a laptop, and a curtain along one wall dividing the room in half, with a fitness room on the other side of the curtain containing an exercise bike and wall mounted Holovision that showed scenery going along as he rode on his bike.

He caught himself staring into space, half wondering about the eerie writing dream, and trying to remember what was on the front cover of the journal.

"Holonet on," he said out loud and the small bar on the desk shot out a laser qwerty keyboard in front of him, while 2 beams of light similar to the holovision box met in the middle to show a rotating globe with the words *Web 3.0* around the circumference, and the familiar DevanderTech logo written on the panel.

DevanderTech

"Search... erm..." The holonet screen showed a big magnifying glass to one side over the rotating globe where the moon would be, and the holo-earth slowed its rotation as if awaiting the next instruction.

"Search for... glow in the dark ink". The magnifying glass stayed where it was as the earth rotated faster, and a couple of seconds later a video somersaulted into the screen in front of the globe.

Not the right one, he thought to himself. After it played, Zac saw millions of results.

"Hmm…. Search for…" The results window closed, and the globe hovered frozen in midair with a magnifying glass to one side, as he racked his brain trying to figure out the right search term to use.

"Search for… invisible ink" Zac commanded the machine. The globe spun again and a few options flipped into view.

Scanning the list of results, he pointed at the floating icon with his finger and went to the MuseoOnline.com holosite for results about papers, inks, and more.

The MuseoOnline.com holosite looked just like a book, and he recognised the swipe interface straight away. Waving his hand from right to left, he gestured to the machine, and the website showed an animation of a hand turning a page.

On the right-hand side of the book, he saw some lettered tabs, marked from A to Z.

Poking his finger at the hologram, he stabbed at the letter I and spotted lots of articles about the history of inks. He read an interesting article, not related, bookmarked it and swiped upward to suggestions of Paper, Pens, Writing, Cryptography, Calligraphy and more.

"Ooh, cryptography" Zac's eyes lit up as he poked at the link and watched videos of the history of cryptography, spies, encryption and other exciting stuff.

He had done research before when looking for books, journals and other protected sources for the shop, but none of it had been this exciting. This was lots of fun and he was learning so much and quite thrilled with what he had found.

As he stared at the screen, he learnt about different invisible inks, from the stuff that children would use like writing with lemon juice and warming up the paper to view the result, to advanced techniques about the way the banks used to watermark their money to prevent counterfeiting, a crime that was no longer an issue since the government banned the use of coinage and notes, and ID-Fobs were the mandatory thing.

He drifted a little off-topic by watching a few videos recommended at the bottom of the article about the greatest robberies back in the day, and the protection devices that banks used when transporting large loads of cash. Zac soon got back on topic, reading about the advances made with a special invisible ink that exploded all over the thief and the money, only viewable under a special light.

He was about to dismiss the article when a word caught his gaze… "orange".

He read more. Perhaps this was it, the orange invisible ink in his dream, and as he investigated further he discovered it, the revelation that blew his mind.

Tucked right at the bottom of the page was a short article that read *Back in the year 2012, criminal investigators used special dye packs that exhibited a controlled explosion of invisible ink that glowed orange under black light.* To protect the money from damage, it gave authorities a sure-fire way to catch the thief by shining a black light on the cash, giving off a bright orange glow, rendering the culprit recognisable, and the cash still in a usable state saving the insurance companies untold millions in pay-outs.

He read that the company which sold these special inks had to change the purpose of their product, when the trees became a protected species, and paper money faded out. To adapt to the loss of invisible ink money protection, the company changed the colour of their inks to green and repurposed it for safety with Fire Protection and Evacuation systems, hence its name FPE paint, or evac-green, as the company called it.

He thought about it, and suddenly….

"Blacklight!" He said it so loudly in his head that other

people would have heard it leaking from his nostrils if they had been sitting next to him.

As his brain went through the events of that night, he remembered the fire alarm had gone off, nothing special about that, it was always some annoying teen or punk who thought it was funny, but what was important was that the safety protocols switched the black lights on when the alarm sounded, In the black light, the green safety paint would glow to show the way to the exits.

Immediately he got out of his chair and went to his toolkit with its specialist tools for antique books. The glues, book-binding materials, special papers, inks, and finally the thing he had been looking for, his little torch with ultraviolet LED and black light. He blew the dust off it and switched it on. It glowed with a dim purple. Grabbing the journal, he opened the book and pointed the purple glow at the blank page, and the words lit up bright orange, along with drawings and other notes.

"YES!" he shouted in excitement.

He put the handle of the torch in his mouth and held the book with both hands.

As he turned the first page, he read.

"Dear Zac..."

Surprised there was nothing else on the first page, curiosity got the better of him. He flipped the page, and there was only one word on it. "If..."

He stared at the page in disbelief. Had he missed something? He shook the torch, switched it off and back on again. Nothing changed. The word if was the only word on the page.

He turned the page again.

"... you are reading this, you have your torch in your mouth, the date is the 22nd of May 2042 and the time is roughly 8:12 am."

Zac checked his watch.

"What the...?"

"How?"

"Oh crap, I'm late for work,".

He triple-clicked the ID fob for his taxi and changed his shirt.

CHAPTER 8

The day at work dragged slowly, the worst he had ever experienced. Zac had always loved it here at Libros Antiques, and never even considered it as work. Since the first day, he volunteered with Old Jim Frade, every single day never felt like work, and he couldn't believe he got paid for doing this dream job... except for today.

This morning's glimpse at the book, that curious book, had got him excited, and he wanted to read more.

He had so many questions. Who had written the orange glowing writing? Could it be possible that they wrote it to him? How did the writer know the exact time and date that Zac would read it, or that he would have his torch in his mouth? How could someone write in it without him knowing?

There were so many questions, and he simply could not wait to get back home and read more.

He daren't take it to work with him, so before he left the house, he locked it up in the safe at his flat.

By the time he closed the shop, he had only sold 3 books, so he locked up early to escape the boredom, and used it as an excuse to get home to the journal.

Even the taxi seemed to go slower today.

When he finally arrived at the building where he lived, he almost ran up the stairwell in excitement, missing every second step.

Arriving at his flat, he swiped the ID fob unlocking the front door, and after opening it, he stopped and stared.

Something was wrong. The plant on the table in the hallway was on the floor, with its pot broken and earth spilt onto the carpet. All the doors along the hallway were open. He walked along the corridor towards the living room; he spotted the coffee table upturned, cushions from the sofa pulled apart, and the stuffing was thrown everywhere.

All the cupboard doors in the kitchen were open, and everything was strewn across the bioplastic lino.

Opening the fridge, Zac grabbed a beer, and then called the police.

The police came and went, taking a statement, retrieving the doorlock logs, and issuing a software security patch to the door lock. Zac was told there had been a spate of thefts in the area, with a Fob cloner, so he would have to go on a waiting list, and they advised him to upgrade his locks.

This was not good. The PHPC agent needed Zac's license fee, and his hardware wallet with its digital coins in it had also gone.

Several hours later, the flat was back in some sort of liveable condition and he had even rehung the broken cupboard door in the kitchen.

In the office, the computer was untouched because of its bio-security controls. No self-respecting thief even bothered to grab a computer these days, they were so traceable, it simply wasn't worth the hassle, and it was so old, it wasn't worth anything anyway.

In the office cupboard, he slid open the curtain and looked disappointedly at the space where his exercise bike had been.

'*Honestly, people would nick anything not screwed down*' he thought to himself.

The rug on the floor was still there, and he pulled it back to reveal the floor safe.

Grabbing the book, and his expensive whiskey from the hole in the floor, he headed to the living room and sat on the rest of the sofa to read.

After a few minutes of reading, the wrist phone vibrated, and he answered it, sticking his finger in his ear.

"Hello?" he sounded his best to appear upbeat, but his brother knew him too well.

"Okay, what happened?" Asked Dylan.

They chatted about the break-in, and life for a while, and then the conversation ended.

"If there's anything I can do for you bro, please get in touch and let me know."

"Will do, thanks for helping me feel better," replied Zac as he hung up.

He picked up the book. There was nothing on the outside, or inside of it, except the scribbles that he wrote as a child. The orange writing had vanished.

Then he remembered the black light, and got to work, replacing the light bulb in the torch. Grabbing the barrel of the torch with his lips, and steadying it with his teeth, he switched it on, and the entire book of secrets came to life.

He fist-pumped the air and then sat down and carried on reading the Professor's notes.

"If you could predict the future, would you want to?" he read.

"Sometimes life is not about what you can see, but what you can't."

"What I am about to tell you is important to the world as you know it. But first, there are some rules."

"1. Never show this book to anyone else or reveal its contents,"

"2. You do not know, what you do not know."

"3. You must help us Zac, to find out the truth of what happened to your father,"

What happened to my father? Who was this guy? How did he come across my journal? How does he know me? What does he know about my parents? There are way too many circumstances and unanswered questions here. Zac's mind was going into overdrive with all the questions.

He carried on reading and looking at the many pictures, maps, and technical drawings. There was a lot of maths that he didn't understand, and some instructions. The more he read, the more he knew the Professor's journal was intended, for him.

As he leafed through the pages, it became more apparent to him that the Professor knew what happened to his father, and Zac had to find out.

The house phone rang, but he was so involved with reading the Professor's journal, he let the answering machine get it.

It was Agent Santelle with an update on payment methods, and a request for Zac to call her back at the earliest chance.

With every page he turned, he learned more and more about the Professor's work, and he got almost a third of the way through, when the torch battery went flat, instantly hiding the Professor's handwritten notes. There was a second of silence, and in a moment of sheer brilliance, he had an idea.

He looked up at the ceiling, then shifted his gaze to the emergency lighting next to the main bulb. Within a few minutes, he replaced the normal lightbulb in his bedroom with the emergency black light.

"Lights on" he called out. The orange writing on his journal lit up again, and he carried on reading the Professor's notes.

The book contained some information about a secret laboratory, and Zac spotted some more maths equations. Whilst turning the page, a loose piece of paper fell out of the book, onto the floor.

Upon inspection, he noticed the paper was a map and picked it up to examine it further. The map showed the local area of Newhaven, the boundary, the cave, and the old hospital between Newhaven and his birth town of Kister-wich, which included a detailed layout of the town drawn up before the disaster. There was a red outline of the new border, with some scribbles showing the differences between before and after the flood. Red circles highlighted Glenbrook Abbey, the old cinema, and the well, and a large red square outline showed the military fence with the letter K in the middle of it, and Zac realised that the scribbles showed the difference between pre-flood Kisterwich and the post-flood town.

Flicking through the book, he noticed a list of items the Professor had written, to help Zac with the journey.

Zac sat quietly and contemplated. There wasn't much for him here in Newhaven. Someone had trashed his place, work was going to be hard now that he had to find more money to pay the PHPC, and to be honest, what else was there, apart from his brother? He needed to do something, and he was curious to find out what happened to his father.

To find the items on the list, Zac opened the storage closet next to the office. To his amazement, the thieves had not raided this room. The vacuum cleaner was still in its same spot, along with the brushes and brooms. His coat was still hanging up, and his toolbox was on the floor, still locked. Next to the toolbox was a battered old storm box, something of a relic from the days when his father had lived in the coun-tryside, filled with necessities such as glow sticks, a small gas stove, and some tins of beans. Zac filled the rest of the back-pack with items from the list and put fresh batteries into the torch.

To get to the laboratory the Professor had written about;

he needed to go on a journey. Zac sat down and read some more, then he read a rather strange sentence. It simply said... "lean forward". *"Lean forward,"* he thought to himself. What could that possibly mean? So he did. As he leant forward, he felt a slight tug on the back of his neck, and the ID fob lurched forward and stuck to the book.

That's weird, he thought to himself.

He pulled on the ID fob and it detached itself from the spine. *Magnetic? What could it be sticking to?* He thought.

Curiously, he opened up the book, the spine gaped open, and a key slid out onto the floor.

Zac picked it up, examined it for a moment, and put it in his pocket, wondering to himself what it was for. Driven by the possibility that his father might still be alive, Zac hunted around his flat for all the stuff he needed for his break away from home.

He grabbed an old green backpack he had used when he was on the backpacking holiday with his brother a few years ago, some rope, leather gloves, the glow sticks from the storm tin, and a bunch of other stuff on the Professors list, including more torch batteries, and a couple of BerryPop bars. Slinging the half-filled pack over his shoulder, he grabbed the journal and went to the front door.

Every page he turned, he learned more and more about the Professor's work and came across more pictures, lists, mathematical equations, and journal entries that described an experiment.

A cloning experiment!

Zac spotted several pages of complex mathematics stuff he simply didn't understand.

This looked like it could be the adventure he was looking for, a chance to escape from the humdrum of life, and find out what happened.

CHAPTER 9

Zac's wrist vibrated, and the display on his Luminettes showed that it was his brother calling.

"Hey Dylan, what's up?" He asked.

"Where are you bro?" he asked impatiently. "I've been at Luigi's waiting for you, and the staff are getting fed up with me not ordering food. I've only had beer and breadsticks."

"Dylan, I'm so sorry. I got distracted. You will never guess what happened... someone broke into my apartment and cleaned me out." Replied Zac.

"Oh man, that sucks. Want me to come over?"

"I've got a better idea. Can you meet me by the old cave in 25 minutes?".

"It's nearly midnight. Are you sure?"

"No questions, just be there, and don't tell anyone."

"Okay bro, I'll just pay the bill, and meet you there."

It was dark outside, and the slight breeze was cold on his face. Zac put on the balaclava, rolling it like a beany, and his luminettes adjusted their night vision. As he strolled through the town's streets, he crept through the shadows so as not to attract attention.

Turning left down the alleyway, after the ChickPick Take-away, Zac squeezed through the gap in the fence behind the bins, to a backyard away from the security cameras in the main street. Slowly he made his way to the copse at the back of the houses and blended into the dark of the night.

He hopped over the fence and onto Edoc Moor, then walked slowly, keeping to the sides, so he didn't get caught in the boggy marsh. As he walked, he remembered something from his childhood. He and his best mate Evan had to be rescued because Evan had dared him to jump from one part to another, and as he jumped, he ended up losing his shoes in the gooey mud. Both he and Evan had got well and truly stuck. Thankfully though, he learned from his mistakes in the past and knew the best parts to walk on.

Venturing further towards the cave, he noticed the moon's light getting brighter, and the luminettes adjusted themselves accordingly.

Coming up to the cave, the light of the moon was blocked by some trees and the luminettes turned up to full brightness. Covering the entrance to the cave were signs "Danger: Unstable mine" and "Warning: No Trespassing".

The metal grid blocking the entrance from the bottom to the top had weathered over the years, but it was still in good standing. In the centre was a door-sized metal gate, with a large sturdy lock attached to it. Zac felt around his pockets for the key that had fallen out of the book's spine, and slipped it into the locks chambers, then turned the key. To his surprise, the lock snapped open and fell onto the floor with a clatter. The sound made him jump, and he turned around to see if anyone was watching him, wondering if someone would spot him at any moment. Nothing moved, no sound, nobody. The surrounding place was silent except for the wind rustling gently in the trees and the sound of crickets.

He waited a few moments, and happy with the fact that no one was there, pushed the gate open. It creaked and groaned as he walked into the cave.

A noise made his heart beat fast, and he turned his head towards it. Dylan was walking down the road, waving a torch around, and humming to himself.

"Hey. Dylan" he whispered loudly.

"What's up, bro?" He shined the torch up at his brother's face, half-blinding him. Zac pushed the torch down gently, and told Dylan about the Professor's journal, as they walked into the cave together.

"So you're telling me that Dad is alive?" Asked Dylan.

"According to this book, yes" replied Zac. He told Dylan about the letter, the timings, and various other things that were more than just coincidence.

"Is that why your flat got robbed bro?"

"I think so, and that's why I know there is something about this. Whoever is behind this, tried to make it look like a robbery, but the journal mentions the robbery too. It's more than coincidence."

Dylan nodded in agreement, pulled an apple out of his pocket, and crunched into it. They carried on walking further into the cave.

The lack of light in the dark cave meant the luminettes weren't working at full power, so Dylan pulled out the torch, switched it on, and blinded them both, as the luminettes light amplification overpowered their eyes. Pointing the torch downwards, Dylan blinked the luminettes off, instantly relaxing his eyes, and got accustomed to the dark once more.

"Bah, I wish they would fix this glitch," said Zac

"Sorry Bro" whispered Dylan.

The light of the torch flickered around the nooks and crannies of the cave, and as they ventured further in, the surrounding sounds got quieter, as if someone had cupped their ears. Standing still, they bathed in silence for a moment. The rustle of the trees, the wind and the chirp of the crickets were no longer there. Each step they took forward, echoed against the cave walls, as both of them went further into the dark unknown. Dylan regained his senses, and the sounds of crunching on gravel and small rocks on the cave floor became louder with every footstep.

There was a rustling noise ahead of them, which got louder and louder, no… closer and closer, and Zac ducked, just before what seemed like a thousand bats, flew over his head, and exited the cave into the midnight sky.

"Damn bro, you could've warned me," said Dylan, scraping some bat poop off his jacket.

"I didn't know that was going to happen," Zac said, silently chuckling to himself.

Zac, his heart beating fast with the unexpected bat flyby, caught his breath and leaned down to grab the torch.

The walls closed in and narrowed as they walked onward into a carved-out tunnel with wooden beams, ceilings and walls. The torch picked out the wooden braces holding up the ceiling and strengthening the walls.

Ahead of them, the torch showed a blockage in the tunnel. There had been a cave-in, with lots of boulders blocking the way forward.

Dylan looked at Zac "Well this is a bust, we may as well go back."

Thoughts went through Zac's mind. *What caused the cave-in? What was on the other side? How would he get to the other side?*

"Wait, I have an idea," said Zac, looking at the Professor's journal.

What would the Professor do? After all, he sent Zac down here. Zac thought to himself.

With no other options left, he shrugged his shoulders, tutted to himself, and took the backpack off.

Inside the Journal, the Professor talked about various weird things that Zac didn't understand, and he skimmed those pages, getting through to the map with the numbers.

Number 7 was the Cave, and a drawing with some rocks

on it gave Zac the information he wanted. With the handle of the torch in his mouth, he looked at the text and read it out loud.

The first task is hard,
  to yourself, you have to prove,
  that tearing it down,
  is your next logical move.

"Well duh, that poem means we have to move the rocks," said Dylan.

It seemed obvious, but not exactly what Zac expected. The Professor wanted them to go forward, through the rocks. Zac moved the backpack to one side behind him and perched the journal on top of it.

Zac wriggled his hands into the leather gloves, and Dylan just tugged at the rocks with his bare hands.

They worked together as a team, clearing the rocks from the mound in front of them, to find out what was on the other side. The clatter of each boulder echoed around the cave as they moved each one from the blockage. Although they were small and took relatively no effort to move, it still felt like at least an hour later before there was a big enough hole for one of them to wriggle through.

As Zac pulled away the rock he was holding, Dylan shone the torch through the hole, and the beam of light lit up the other side of the tunnel. Through the small opening in the rocks, he could see that the rest of the tunnel was clear.

Zac put the journal in his pocket, then squeezed the rucksack through the hole, and slid in through the rocks on his stomach, pushing the rucksack in front of him.

Placing both hands on the floor, and his chest still laid on the rocks, he pulled himself forwards, scraping his knees and legs on the floor with a thud as he climbed out. After dusting himself off, he walked along the brick tunnel.

Looking through the opening at his brother, he asked, "Are you coming?"

"Yea, yea, just need to grab a few more rocks out of the way, and I will be with you in a moment," replied his brother.

As his brother made a larger opening, Zac flickered the torch around. It was the same as before, except that the ground had changed from dust and rubble to smooth bricks, each footstep echoing along the tunnel. Dylan squeezed himself through to where Zac was, and they carried on along the tunnel. As they walked, Zac looked at the neat brickwork as the beam of his torch flickered from left to right. Walking further into the pitch black, the floor seemed to become more difficult to see, and what Zac thought was his eyes playing tricks on him, suddenly became real as the dark expanse beneath him turned out to be a hole in the floor.

Within moments, he felt his legs buckle beneath him as he hit the floor, and gravity took the rest of his body with it.

"Woah Bro, are you okay down there?" Asked Dylan in the darkness.

Zac lay on his front, the wind knocked out of him, and stayed still, doing a mental check on all his bodily systems.

Did anything hurt? Where did it hurt? Could he move?

Looking up, he saw the faint light of the tunnel he had come from.

"Yea, I'm fine". Came the reply.

He moved his head a little, then a few fingers and his knees, slowly pushing his hands against the floor, rolling himself over onto his back.

"Stay there, I'm going to get someone to help. I would come down, but if we both get stuck, that's stupid."

"Okay, Dylan" called Zac.

"I'll be back as soon as possible."

Zac listened as more rocks clattered, and he heard Dylan's

footsteps getting quieter as his brother walked down the tunnel into the darkness.

Zac flicked on the black-light torch, and sitting up, he pulled the journal out of his pocket, turning to the page with the map on it.

The scratchily drawn map contained some fairly intricate details.

He looked closely at the numbers related to some of the text in the book. Flicking from page to page confirmed that he was right. The numbers were a simple form of a key.

1 was the cave gate, 2 was the lock, 3 pointed at what looked like an entrance to the boundary of what he assumed was Kisterwich, as it had a large K in the centre of the square, and some more numbers referenced the well, the old Glenbrook Abbey, and more.

There were ten numbers altogether.

Zac got up and walked forward to find a way out. A faint smell wafted through the air, and he wondered what it might be.

Reading through the pages of the Professor's journal, Zac found the next clue.

When the road ahead is empty,
   and you cannot clearly see,
   plunge yourself into darkness,
   then you can follow me.

Zac waved the torch around but couldn't see anything. He switched it off, hoping that something might glow, but nothing happened.

"Great, what am I supposed to do now?" He thought. He flashed the torch over the book and read the clue again. The smell was stronger now, and the cereal bar had done nothing for his hunger. "Plunge yourself into darkness" he kept repeating over and over in his head. "Plunge, plunge, plunge?". "Darkness, darkness, darkness?". His brain was fried, and his stomach grumbled, he was feeling cold and tired. He couldn't go backward, so the only way was forward, but how? With the handle of the torch in his mouth, he looked through his rucksack and tried to work out what each piece of equipment might be for.

Rope? no idea,

Blacklight? obviously for reading the diary,

Leather gloves? he was already wearing these, and they had helped him while moving the rocks,

Other stuff? he hadn't found a use for yet.

Creativity flowed, and his brain came up with some weird ideas for the different equipment. He carried on following the maps instructions, and they lead him down the small tunnel into a large cavern. As he stepped into the expanse, he could hear drips of water and the echo of his footsteps, and there was also a temperature change, as it got noticeably warmer.

Looking at the book, he realised the clue wasn't about the darkness of the cave, but the darkness of black light. Pressing the button of the black light, he waved it around and saw a few flecks of glow in the blackness.

"Yes", he shouted and punched the air. His voice echoed around the cave.

Excited he had found a solution to the clue, he blinked to activate the luminettes low-light vision and the flecks of glow from the black-light paint became clearer.

The blurred lines he had seen became small arrows as he got closer to them. He followed the arrows on the floor until he came to a wall and spotted the words "press here" daubed in paint. With an arrow pointing to a curious-looking outcrop of rock.

He ambled across the floor and pushed the stone into the wall. A thin beam of light appeared, defining the outside of the stone, and with a click, it slid away from him into the wall, and then glided upwards revealing a keypad.

Why was there a keypad inside a wall of a cave? he thought. He checked the journal for a code, but only saw another annoying riddle.

Hungry, you must be.
  To see the bright blue sky,
  To proceed you must now input,
  The first 6 slices of Pi

Mmmm Pie, he thought, as his stomach rumbled. It had felt like hours since he had eaten, and he remembered the second Berry-pop bar in his backpack.

Munching on the cereal bar, he hadn't realised just how hungry he was.

The darkness of the cave, and the overwhelming flood of that strange smell, really messed with his senses. His stomach growled some more. The cave wall shone with a strange swirl of colours as if the shadows were coming to life. Some small indistinguishable shapes appeared at first.

He squinted his eyes and concentrated, and the shapes became bits of food. First, he saw his favourite ChickPick meal. It was doing a slow waltz with a dinner plate and a carving knife, then a nice frosty glass of lemonade, complete with straw, which was juggling ice cubes, and a steaming pie, just glowing on the wall, with a slice missing.

He saw the pie's ingredients, like a giant list. 4 pounds of beef, 3 and a half cups of beef stock, 1 pound of mushrooms, 1 chopped onion, 1 and a half cups of flour, 1 egg and 1 pound of frozen pastry (thawed). The numbers and words moved around. He rubbed his head. It was still sore from the bump when he had fallen through the hole in the floor, but it wasn't bleeding.

What was going on? Is he dead, or was he unconscious? He wondered, *What was in this cereal bar? Why was he in the cave? What was that smell?*

Then he saw a shadow and suspecting someone might be behind him, he turned around, but no one was there. Looking back at the wall, he watched in disbelief as he saw a school tie, a pocket on a blazer, and some white teeth smiling. More features became clearer, and he recognised that the drawing on the wall was of his school friend Darren. Darren opened his mouth and started mumbling, the sort of mumble you hear when you're not listening to someone. Zac focussed on what Darren was saying, but it made no sense at all. Then he said something very clearly.

"Guess what, I know pie to three point one four slices".

Zac's stomach growled as Darren ate the Pie. Crumbs fell out of Darren's mouth, and the numbers followed them. Darren picked them up and started juggling with the numbers. Zac watched as each number bounced around in circles, and then Darren grabbed a number and hurled it at Zac.

The shadows, the weird daydreams, that smell! His senses were completely overwhelmed; Zac fell backwards as if the number had hit him. Sat on the floor, Zac looked up at Darren. The number 3 was about a metre high, and Zac's bookshop knowledge told him the font was probably 1000 times New Roman. Behind it, Darren was still juggling.

It was almost as if there was a sheet of glass between him and Zac, and the metre-long 3 was sticking to the glass. Like a fast bowler, Darren keenly eyed the plate, then pulled his arm up and wound up for the fast bowl. His arm spun around like a helicopter blade getting faster and faster, and then, he let go. The dot of a number grew larger and larger hurtling towards Zac, and he flinched expecting the number to break through the invisible window, but it didn't. Instead, it stopped just as before.

More and more numbers came one after another. He looked up at Darren and realised… 3.1415926. It was Pi! It was the value of Pi to the first six places, not slices of Pie.

Now he understood. Zac stood up and instantly, the drawing of Darren, and all the other things just ran down the wall, as if dripping like wet paint, and just like that, Zac was in the darkness again, with only the light of the keypad to keep him company.

He walked to the wall. As he thumbed each button of the keypad, a red light glowed, and then a green glow showed the end of the sequence. With a heavy mechanical clunk, the door unlocked, confirming he had got the correct code.

All around him, he could hear the clunking sounds of large cogs, grinding, and crunching as they turned and the rock wall to his left slowly moved backwards, spilling dust and dislodging some cobwebs.

An enormous spider scuttled its way along the floor.

Zac walked into the room as the large rock door slid open, releasing more dust from the cracks in the wall. In front of him was a long passageway which didn't look at all like the cave. Instead, it was an arched brick tunnel barely 2 feet across, and approximately 8 feet high with strip lights above him. This tunnel reminded him of the places he used to go with his dad on ghost walks when he was a boy.

The bottoms of his shoes clicked against the cobbled floor, echoing down the tunnel, and as he ventured further, motion-activated lights flickered on, half blinding him, and catching him by surprise. At the end of the bricked corridor, the narrow walls opened up into a larger, more cave-like-looking room with some army issue backpacks packed with supplies.

Attached to the wall, near the entrance of the room were some special yellow laboratory-style containment suits. They reminded Zac of the ones he had seen on TV, which emergency services wore after the collapse of the dam to prevent the spread of diseases.

Over in the corner was another door, and a big green exit sign brightly lit.

He pushed open the door and looked outside, waiting for a moment for his eyes to adjust.

CHAPTER 10

This was an unfamiliar landscape, nothing he was used to, back in Newhaven. He hadn't experienced anything like this in decades. There were no tall towers, no cameras, no bustling crowds, no warm electric smells, no humming of motors, just quiet and nothingness.

The first thing he noticed was the cool breeze of the outside air brushing against his face, and it was a welcome relief from the stuffiness and dampness of the cave. As he ventured out, he buttoned up his jacket to keep out the cold and pulled the balaclava beany over his ears. The wet road in front of him reflected the light of the moon. There were silhouettes of trees to his left, and mountains on the right, disappearing into the distance.

Although his skin was cold, the luminettes had enough power to give him the enhanced night vision he had become accustomed to. Looking at the journal, he regarded the hand-drawn map and smiled at how accurate it had been so far. As he scanned the drawing, he compared it to the landscape in front of him. Behind him was the letter H, and the cave. In front of him, were rocks as far as the eye could see, a winding road, a cross, and further on was a big letter K with an arrow, and the number 39 next to it. Zac flicked to page thirty-nine and confirmed that this was the page number for the next map.

In front of him was a road that turned the corner, carving a track through the hills towards the horizon. To the right of him, the other end of the road disappeared into the darkness. In the distance, there was the sound of running water, and Zac assumed this was the river he could see on the map. Behind him, there was a loud clunk, and he turned around to find the door was closed. He tried opening it, but it was no good, it simply wouldn't budge.

Something caught his eye, and he noticed an insect scuttling up the side of the door. Zac looked up and saw the top of the cave, and the rocks above it jutting into the sky. One minute he was in Newhaven, the next, he was in a cave, and now he was in a foreign land, with an empty road. What the heck was going on? He couldn't go back to the cave, the urge to go forward was too great. *What was there? What did the Professor want him to see?*

He walked down the road and glanced at the map to check where he was.

The quiet night was only interrupted by the sound of the water, which got louder as he walked closer to the big K on the map. Arriving at the highest point of the bridge, Zac leant against the cobbled wall and looked down into the water of the river Glen, watching it flow, and swirl, for a few minutes. The wind started to blow harder against his face.

Further down the road, he walked past a very run-down-looking hospital.

This must be what the cross meant on the map, Zac thought to himself. The sign said "Kisterwich General Hospital". It looked derelict, the main doors were hanging open, and windows were smashed.

Zac stared into the darkness and could see tufts of grass poking through the concrete in the car park, with rubble, a spare wheel, broken bottles, and the remains of an ambulance that had been picked clean of anything of worth.

Metal barricades surrounded the building. Large signs warned people to stay away, and *"Danger of death"*. Zac carried on towards a large dark area populated by trees. In the darkness, he could make out his old hometown, with houses, trees, some other buildings, and the outline of the top of the barbed wire fencing surrounding the entire area.

Something caught his attention, a beam in the darkness, swaying from left to right, a searchlight coming from the compound. He remembered what the book had said.

Continuing on
  The route that is right
  Keep down low
  And stay in the night.

He peered carefully into the darkness and could make out the large abbey, where his mother and father used to take him for Sunday mass. The road led to a large solid barrier, and Zac's luminettes picked up the distinctive yellow and black painted diagonal stripes on it, blocking the road.

As he ventured closer, he noticed a security hut next to the barrier. There was no guard inside it, and Zac wondered if he was the guy on the roof operating the searchlight. But what was he looking for? There was no one else here. Zac waited next to a tree, camouflaged by the darkness.

On Page 39, the map showed some photos stuck to the page and a crudely drawn layout of the town. There were buildings, and trees, the checkpoint, the road, the abbey, and a well on the outside of the wall, close to the abbey, with a dotted line going outside the compound and a big arrow pointing to it.

The searchlight flashed around again, and he instinctively ducked down. Although he was nowhere near, he didn't want to risk being caught.

Following the dotted line on the map, Zac eventually reached the fence, keeping out of the wake of the beam. Attached to the fence, there were large signs warning people to stay out, and "10,000v - Danger of death KEEP OUT"

He squatted next to the well, took off his backpack, and flipped to the next page of the journal.

It talked about a secret passage in the well and advised him to wear goggles, so he grabbed them from the side pocket in his backpack. Zac took off the balaclava and stuffed it inside the bag, then stretched the elastic of the goggles, and placed them over his head so that they dangled around his neck.

The first detail he noticed about the well was the large cobblestones on the outside. On top was a wooden lid that looked like a wagon wheel which Zac had seen in old western movies when he was a child.

Inserting his fingers into the grab holes, he slowly eased up the lid and slid it across the opening to the well. It landed on its side, with a thump on the grass, and he peered into the black abyss.

At approximately 10 feet wide, the inside of the well had brick walls that Zac estimated were at least two feet thick, with a six-foot wide hole leading down into the black.

Pulling out the glow stick from his backpack, he snapped it, shook it, and the glow shone up the surrounding area. Scared that he had given himself away, he dropped it down the well, and after a second or two, there was a quiet splash as it hit the bottom, lighting up the water and the inside of the well with a green glow.

The searchlight switched off and Zac thought he heard the voices of two men talking but couldn't make out what they were saying.

With his eyes getting accustomed to the dark again, Zac looked down into the hole. It looked at least 100 feet deep. The luminettes could make out some gaps in the brickwork at equal spacings from the top of the well downward, towards the bottom. Each gap was the right size for hands and feet.

He tidied everything into the backpack, packed it into the bioplastic bag to waterproof it, and tied the whole thing to the end of the rope.

So far, so good he thought.

Grabbing hold of the pack and the rope Zac slowly lowered it into the well until it was just above the water. With the rope not quite long enough to lower it anymore, he let go and heard the splash as his bag hit the water, closely followed by the coils of rope.

How could I forget to tie this end? He thought to himself.

Easing his body over the side of the well, he lowered himself, feet first, into the hole and stepped into the first foothold. Putting his right foot into the next hole further down, he descended into the well.

Stepping into each foothold, he went deeper and deeper, the leather gloves protecting his hands against the rough brick footholds, as he disappeared into the dark.

Each footstep echoed in the darkness, and as he took each hand and foot out, some debris would fall out of the footholds and drop into the water below, echoing as it hit the water's surface.

Getting closer to the bottom, he noticed the ripples of the water glowing green and the smell of dampness around him getting stronger.

With less than ten feet to go, as he moved his left hand downwards, he slipped on a moss-covered brick, lost his grip and fell into the water beneath him.

Water enveloped him, and as he went under, he panicked as the pressure against his chest knocked the air out of his lungs. Instinct drew him upwards towards the floating stick of glowing green, his arms flailed, and his legs kicked frantically.

As his face broke through the surface of the water, Zac opened his lungs to breathe in the air.

Treading water in the glow stick light, he quickly became comfortable with his new surroundings.

Zac remembered that the Professor's book mentioned an entrance somewhere here.

But where was it?

He swam around in a circle trying to push the old bricks to reveal a secret door or wall, but nothing happened.

Then he had a spark of an idea.

Stretching the elastic from around his neck, he placed the goggles over his eyes, took a breath, and braced himself.

Grabbing the end of the rope, Zac tied it around his waist. With a glow stick in one hand, he breathed in slowly, filling both lungs with air, then swam downwards.

The glow stick lit up the floor underneath the water and it wasn't too long before Zac spotted an arch-shaped entrance.

He let out all the air in his lungs in excitement and swam upwards to the well opening to grab some more air.

After filling his lungs with more oxygen, he dived again.

Through his goggles, he spotted the archway in the wall beneath the water and headed towards it. The underwater tunnel led upwards at an angle away from the main well, and towards some steps. Emerging from the water, climbing the stairs, and out of the pool, Zac breathed in the air once again and rested for a moment to take another breath to regain his energy.

Next, he pulled on the rope attached to his backpack, dragging it along the same route, through the passage, and out of the water, and placed it next to himself on the floor.

Dripping wet, and feeling quite cold by now, he opened the bioplastic bag and looked through the backpack, hoping to find something to dry himself with.

Opening the Professor's journal, Zac cracked another glow stick, hanging it around his neck, and read using the black light torch.

Stuck to the page of the journal was a blueprint of the Abbey. On top of the blueprints was some tracing paper with a crudely drawn diagram of the route which ended with an X. On the next page, the Professor had written some history of the abbey.

The place you are entering was once a secret tunnel to help people escape from the Nazis during World War 2. Refugees would come into the Abbey, down the stairs into the crypt towards the hidden exits behind the wine shelves, and on through the tunnels. They would sit in the waiting area until dark before escaping through the well and away from the Germans. You will find some clothes, get changed, and then proceed along the tunnel.

Zac saw a long corridor in front of him, and the Professors writings reminded him of a feint memory or two of that history lesson at school that he should have paid more attention to, instead of staring out of the window, looking at the cloud shapes as they floated through the sky.

As he walked down the long corridor, the glow of the light defined every brick in the tunnel and each brick had characteristics and shapes.

The small square room at the end of the tunnel was bare, except for stone benches on either side, a walkway through the middle, and a large fan at the far end of the room, with blades that reached from floor to ceiling.

On the wall next to the fan, Zac found some clothes hung up and then got changed into them.

Looking around the benches, he spotted several names gouged into the walls, names and sentiments encouraging others they were going to be free soon, a sort of "I woz ere" memorial for all the people who had escaped during the war.

The large fan blades were made of rusting metal and easily twice as tall as he was.

Must be some sort of air-conditioning and also the way forward, Zac thought to himself.

Remembering the newspaper clipping, he opened the Professor's journal and read about how the military had moved into Kisterwich after the collapse of the Heyworth Dam.

Next to the clipping, there was a quickly jotted sketch of the route to the X. It showed some sort of ventilation system.

In the notes underneath the article, there was a note scribbled in the Professor's handwriting.

I have disabled the ventilation fan, you need to go through the gaps between the blades until you reach the ducts, then crawl along the ducts and down into the room where your journey ends.

This was it. He was almost at the X, whatever X was. Zac waved the glow stick from left to right slowly, examining the way forward, and walked through the gap between the blades. In front of him was a metal gate firmly locked into place, with a small sign above it that read 'Catacombs 1205ad – 1534ad', and to his right, a slatted grill for the air ducting.

According to the journal, the gate was what the refugees used to escape from the Germans during the war.

Zac quickly got to work with his screwdriver on his multi-function pocket knife, unscrewing the grill. He carefully placed the panel on the floor and leaned it against the wall. The place was eerily quiet, and each turn of the knife echoed down the ducting with a metallic shaft, as it screeched metal against metal.

He pulled himself into the duct, then got onto all fours, crawling forward using his elbows and knees, inch by inch. The duct walls shone green all around him as the metal panels reflected the light from the stick hanging from his neck.

As he made his way forward, the metal panels buckled slightly under his weight and made a sound of bowing and creaking. Ahead of him, the ducting carried on, and on his right, he saw a slatted grill. As he reached it, the glow stick revealed a hinge. Carefully, he nudged himself towards the grill to stay quiet and undetected.

Zac peered through the slits of the grill. The room was in complete darkness.

With a triple-flick of his eyelids, the luminettes activated the enhanced night vision and this time he could see a room decked out with computers and other technical equipment with a large window along one wall.

Convinced that he was in the right place, according to the map, he inspected the grill. Apart from the hinge, there was also the bare metal of a screw holding it in place.

He sat up, with his back against the ducting wall, and feet on the grill. The top of the ducting wasn't quite high enough for him to sit comfortably.

Carefully, and with deliberate movements, he pushed against the grill with his feet, and after a few moments and some slight creaking, the top left corner gave way. He put more pressure on the bottom left corner of the grill with his feet, and it popped open.

He moved into a different position, peeked out of the duct hole and saw that he was directly above the main computer desk, which was only a few feet down.

Turning over onto his stomach, Zac grabbed both sides of the opening with each hand and stuck his feet out of the ducting. Holding onto the sides, he carefully lowered himself onto the computer desk.

The light switched on, blinding him. Losing his balance, he rolled off the table and slammed onto the floor with a thud, and stayed there motionless, his heart almost thumping out of his chest.

Remaining motionless, he looked around, to get his bearings. It was a rectangular room, with desks on the long sides, covered with computer equipment, monitors, touch screens, servers, and keyboards.

There were some pens attached to a large whiteboard, with technical scribbles on it. The logo in the top left corner was from the Devander Corporation.

Zac stayed on the floor, motionless, trying to think.

What would he do if someone came? How would he explain this? Who would they be? What would they want? Surely, he would be in a lot of trouble.

After what felt like five minutes, the light switched off, plunging the room into darkness.

He waited, perfectly still, his side aching from the fall from the table, but there was nothing. No sounds at all.

Was there even anyone here at all? he asked himself.

He stood up, and the light switched on again. In the middle of the room was a sensor on the ceiling, and he noticed that a red LED lit up every time he moved.

Brushing himself off, he got back onto his feet.

Behind the long wall in front of him, with all the computers, was a large observation window, and next to that on the left was a door. The room that the window looked out to was pitch black, and all that Zac could see was his reflection. Cupping his hand against the window and peering in through the glass didn't seem to make a difference either. He looked around for a light switch for the room on the other side of the window but couldn't find one. So, he flicked on the torch, and walked to the door, into the darkness.

Just as before, the lights flickered on. Dazzled by the brightness, he scrunched his eyes closed. The luminettes enhanced night-vision finally powered off, and he opened his eyes.

Zac stood in a large white room. It was square-shaped with large shiny white tiles on the ceilings, walls and floor. In the middle of each wall was a door. The map in the journal described these as the North, South, East and West doors, one of which lead from the computer room he had climbed into.

On his right, he heard a whirring noise, like the noise from a motor, and as he looked up, he saw a security camera staring straight at him. The lens rotated as it focused on him.

The speaker popped, and a relaxing, friendly female voice announced "facial identification in progress".

Zac watched in curiosity.

"Identity confirmed, welcome to Infinity Labs Mr Drummond."

"What the -?"

A shimmering hologram of a man interrupted him. He was clean-shaven, balding, with grey tufts of hair above his ears and wore a blue bowtie, a white shirt, and a white lab coat with lots of pens in the left breast pocket. Tucked under his arm was a clipboard.

"Hello Zac."

CHAPTER 11

"Hello?" He replied in disbelief.

"How? ... What? ... Who are you?".

Zac looked at the hologram and blinked, unsure if it was real or not. He was used to seeing holograms before, the Holovision, Holonet, and adverts in the streets on billboards, but this hologram was different.

It was a super-high-definition image, and not as translucent as other holograms. If he hadn't seen it flicker in front of him, he could mistake it for an actual person. This was next-level tech.

Zac paused for a moment taking it in, but there were so many questions, he didn't know where to start. He stood staring at it.

"You are probably wondering who I am, what this place is, and how I know you," started the old man.

"My name is Professor Eric Mullins, and this is my super-high definition hologram. I have programmed it, to be as interactive as possible, so I can respond to any questions you may have. Hopefully, my artificial intelligence can help you, simply by talking to it... er... me. If you require more in-depth knowledge, please ask me for a menu, and the list of choices will help you find what you are looking for."

A small menu appeared in a rectangle in front of the Professor, scrolled through some choices, and then disappeared.

Zac nodded, then realised that the hologram probably couldn't see him. The Professor said, "Good, now we can continue".

Surprised by the hologram's response, he asked, "Okay, first question, did you just see me nod?"

"Of course, the security camera watches for your movements, facial expressions, gestures and body language, and that information is received by my hologram."

"Wow, that's impressive," replied Zac.

"How does the computer know who I am?"

"We have met before, 30 years ago," the Professor continued.

This confused Zac, he didn't remember meeting any scientists when he was 10, and besides, 30 years ago he was just a schoolchild. These days Zac had a goatee and glasses now, and was almost twice as tall, so how could the security camera know who he was?

"What is this place?"

"This is infinity Labs, the place of infinite possibilities, and we create new inventions for the world, and sometimes the Military," replied the old man.

"Such as?"

"The Luminettes you are wearing, we created those, and holovision, the holonet, glow rings, manklets, the GPS-taxis, the interactive mirrors, and fake windows, hover bikes, the heat exchanger chip that goes into your Wristphone5 to make it use your body heat to run it, and much more."

"More?"

"Some things, you can't explain, you just have to experience to understand," said the Professor.

Confused by the answer, Zac asked another question.

"Why have you bought me here, what do you want me to do?"

"We need your help,"

"Who's we?"

"I'm sorry, I don't understand the question, please use the menu function for more information."

"Menu."

"The following subjects are available for discussion, People, Places, Events."

"Erm... People."

"There are several sections in this category... Family, Friends, School, The Lab, more."

Although he wanted to find out more about the people in the lab, his immediate thoughts went to someone much closer.

"Mum," He blurted out.

"Would you like to hear general information or current Information?"

"Everything, tell me all of it," said Zac.

"Rebecca Louise, born Rebecca Louise King on 11th August. She grew up in Kisterwich where she fell in love with Michael Drummond, they became high school sweethearts and married. She is the mother to James Isaac Drummond, also known as Zac, and his brother Dylan Jeffrey Drummond." The hologram continued, with stories about the life of his mother.

Zac smiled as he heard the good things about her. It was a loving story that his mother and father had told countless times. How they became high school sweethearts, their perfect life, and how destiny had brought them together.

The Professor interrupted Zac's calming thoughts, with the latest information.

"She was arrested on 3rd Nov 2008 for the destruction of the Heyworth Dam on 21 May 2008, and all the lives it claimed. Now in a chemically induced coma for the rest of her life as a punishment for her crimes."

"Do you wish to know more information?"

"No" Zac snapped, remembering the evil that she had done. The countless lives lost that day, the way she denied it, even though there was photographic evidence, video evidence, and witness testimony at the trial.

Zac listened as the Professor explained how Zac's father and he used to work together, back when his father was in the military.

Dad had spoken about his service to the country but mentioned nothing about the Professor.

He quizzed the Professor for more information, but the hologram just answered with a short statement.

"Sorry, that's classified."

"So, why am I here?" Zac asked with a confused look on his face.

"And what's with all the cloak and dagger?"

"You are here because your father and I came across a secret project that created the unthinkable. A chance to stretch the boundaries of science and experience things only ever dreamt of before."

Zac couldn't believe it. Even though he hadn't got a clue what the hologram was talking about, he was in complete awe of whatever was going on. The confusing thing was, that although the Professor had completely intrigued the young man, he hadn't given any details about whatever it was, and Zac was still clueless.

"Before we continue, I need to take a bio imprint of you, so that we can check if you are compatible." Said the Professor, directing Zac's gaze to the tables in the middle of the room.

"Bio Imprint"? He asked with a look of confusion on his face.

"Yes, we use it to unlock the machine, and help you learn the secrets of the past, present and future."

"And this will help me find out what happened to my dad?" Zac asked.

The Professor's hologram paused and then repeated itself.

"Okay, okay, so how do I do it?" Zac asked, getting impatient with all the security procedures.

"Just lie down on the TripleScan machine, and I will do the rest." A shimmering opaque hologram of the Professor laid down on the table to show Zac, then faded as Zac approached the table.

Expecting it to be cold to the touch, Zac carefully sat down in the centre of the TripleScan. He was pleasantly surprised at how warm the table was, and as he swung around, he laid his feet into position on the end of the table, and laid his head onto the shiny metal surface, contoured for his neck and spine.

"Okay, done. What now?" Asked Zac, not sure what to expect.

The Professor's brightness dimmed to 25%, and he stepped back. The lights dimmed, and a bright holographic rectangular screen appeared in front of him.

Zac watched in interest as a video played.

"Since the dawn of man, we have made mistakes, and often wished we could go back and erase them. People have theorised it, stories written about it, but we here at Infinity Laboratories have created the prototype."

"The prototype of what?" Interrupted Zac.

"This prototype of the Living Another Timeline Machinery." The video paused as the Professor waited, expecting Zac to ask another question.

"That seems like a weird name for the machine" Zac replied with a confused look on his face.

"We were going to call it the Split Point Limited Adventure Travel, but shortening it down to SPLAT seemed silly, so, it's the Living Another Timeline Machine, which we here affectionately know as LATiMer." Explained the Professor.

The video carried on, explaining how the Professor thought up the project, and how it was supposed to be all about a faster way to make clones. When the video had finished, the Professor told Zac about how the machine works, and that there are rules to travelling in time.

"So, you're telling me you built a way to travel through time?"

"Yes, but we built it differently."

"What do you mean?"

The Professor closed his fist.

The Professor stated the rules of conventional time travel, and as he rattled off each rule he extended each finger, counting out the rules as he spoke.

"You cannot occupy the same space at the same time. You can only jump within your lifetime. There are fixed points in time where you can't change anything. If your past self has an injury or is killed, your future self has a healed wound or a gravestone. You can only time travel naked."

Zac pulled a face "Even if this were true, and this machine…"

"Latimer" The Professor interrupted.

"Even if this were true, and Latimer allowed me to travel in time, there is no way I am doing it nude!" remarked Zac.

"Which brings me to my next point" replied the Professor, putting his hands in his pockets.

"These rules are supposed to be written in stone and keep time travellers safe, but…. what if - you could break the rules? Not just one, but all of them. What if - there was a way to achieve all of this?"

"Okay…" Zac paused, a million questions running through his head.

The Professor's hologram paused, and appeared to inhale,

in the same way as someone would before they gave out bad news.

"So what did you mean when you said 'it breaks all the rules' "?

"That's trickier to explain, it's probably easier to show you instead."

The Professor took a few steps backwards, and he faded to fifty per cent brightness. In front of him, a holographic rectangular window appeared, and the video played.

Zac watched the viewscreen. The video explained how time travel is usually theorised as one person being moved completely from one time to another, and all the pitfalls associated with such limited travel.

The viewscreen paused, and the Professor simply said, "But the method used here, is different."

The video resumed, and Zac could see a view from the CCTV camera, of the Professor, and a young woman. Zac watched as she put a piglet on one table. The piglet lay there motionless.

"That's cruel. Why did you kill that poor piglet?"

The video paused.

"It's not dead, merely sedated," replied the Professor.

The video resumed, and an archway fixed to the table, moved from one end of the table to the other, gliding as if on runners.

The next table then did something similar, and the cover slid across to reveal an identical piglet.

"Woah, what just happened? Did you just clone that piglet?"

"I'm glad you asked" replied the hologram.

"Your father and I used existing bio-engineering cloning tech, developed in the 1990s, and applied it differently. Instead of growing the clone over months, we can now 3d print the cloned animal, vegetable or mineral in less than 30 minutes."

"What? But that's impossible," said Zac in complete amazement.

"The test subject is put to sleep and then placed on the TripleScan. This machine contains technology that extracts DNA, X-rays, and a skin scanning technology that is used in airports,"

Zac sat up so he could see the video more clearly.

"Then the data is saved as a complex file and kept in the storage capacitors and can be stored. This means the test subject can be cloned, the data stored, and in 20 years, Latimer recreates a clone of the subject, and it then makes a reproduction from that data. The original subject is unharmed."

"So, instead of moving the actual piglet in time, you can send a copy instead?"

"Exactly, and because of this, we can break a few time-travel rules!"

"How?" Asked Zac curiously.

The lights brightened, the rectangular video screen disappeared, the holoprof became 100% visible, and explained.

In normal time travel, if your past self is injured, then your future self will end up with the same injury. However, if your clone is injured, or killed, it doesn't affect you, or vice versa. This is where we break one of the time travel rules.

The airport technology inside Latimer means you can wear clothes, and be scanned, so you don't have to travel in time naked. Another rule is broken.

"That makes sense. So have you travelled through time?" He asked the Professor.

"No, my work here is too important, and besides, the information inside my head is too valuable for me to leave this place," the Professor said, adjusting his glasses.

"How many people have used this machine?" Asked Zac.

"So far" the Professor looked at his notes "One person".

"Who?"

"Sorry, the logs have been wiped, so I can't tell you that."

Zac pulled a face, wondering what that was all about, but the holoprof distracted him with another video.

They chatted for about fifteen minutes, and Zac listened while the Professor talked more about the construction of the machine.

Zac thought about this for a moment.

"You mean, I can go back, or forward in time?"

"Yes, and we want you to go back, to destroy Latimer. If you do this, we will help you find out the truth of what happened to your father."

"Are you kidding me?" Zac said angrily. "I haven't walked all this way for you to show me how to break the very thing that might help me find out the truth. If you want my help, then you need to tell me what happened first!".

The Holoprof paused for a moment, thinking.

"Agreed. But once you have your answers, we destroy the machine".

"So why do I need to destroy it, this thing could do all sorts of good in the world?"

"Someone went back in time, and caused some problems, and now we need to fix them. The only way to do that is to blow up the machine and prevent it from happening in the future."

"I see," said Zac. "But how do I get back?" he asked in a confused tone.

They chatted, and the Professor reminded Zac that he wouldn't go back in time, but Latimer would clone him, and the clone would be sent back through time instead. In his mind, it all clicked into place, and Zac agreed.

The Professor showed him the correct protocol to close the machine, including a safe way to dismantle it, and that his clone would just stay there in the past, grow old and die.

"Aren't you worried about the butterfly effect? You know,

where I do something in the past, and it affects the future?" Asked Zac.

"Not at all. If you read later on in the book you're holding, you will see, that there is no issue here, because the future is not fixed, and can be changed. Another rule of time travel we can break."

"For all we know, someone has already gone back to the past, and changed things already, and maybe helped your mum and dad get together, and you were born," said the Professor with a grin on his face.

"Don't be stupid, that sort of thing only happens in movies," replied Zac.

That did it, he'd decided. He was going back to the past to help the Professor, and find out what happened to his father.

"Menu," said Zac.

The holoprof repeated the choices.

"People, Places, Events, Time-Travel,"

"Time-Travel," said Zac, and he read the choices in the next menu.

"Open Triplescan," he commanded.

The arches on the table to his left slid from the bottom end of the table to the top end, and the holoprof talked him through the procedure, step by step.

It explained how the subject lies down on the table, and how the entire process was harmless.

On the arch, a nozzle extended, positioning itself an inch away from his arm.

There was a quick spray of something cold on his skin, and then Zac lost the feeling in his arm.

"It's okay, this won't hurt a bit," reassured the Professor.

His legs became heavy, and almost straight away, his entire body felt the same. He tried to speak but couldn't move his lips. He couldn't move his head, or his arms, or anything.

A moment of fear swept through Zac as he realised his paralysis left him feeling so vulnerable, and then the first arch rolled along the rails on either side of him, scanning his entire body from head to foot.

Another arch did the same thing, scanning this time with a different coloured light.

The third arch glowed purple and made no noise. Meanwhile, the Professor had put on some classical music in the background to calm Zac, giving him something to focus on, instead of the arches.

He noticed a loud humming noise coming from the capacitor room which grew louder and louder.

The arch finished scanning him, and he noticed that the classical music had increased in volume, to mask the humming.

The humming noise became unbearably loud, and all Zac wanted to do was cover his ears, but he still couldn't move, and the noise became so intense, he felt that he would pass out at any moment. Without warning... the sound ceased, and the lab was plunged into silence.

CHAPTER 12

2 1 May 2008

Zac's eyes opened, and he looked upwards. He was still lying down, and the humming from the capacitor was louder than before. But this time, things were different.

His eyes were sticky, and he could smell bacon.

As he moved his head around, he noticed that the Professor was no longer visible.

The collar of his shirt scratched against his neck, and as he started to move, he noticed that all of his clothes felt odd for some reason, stiffer, as if they were starched, something that Zac would never do.

He sat up. The room looked different, but he couldn't quite put his finger on it.

Had it worked? Had he travelled to the past?

This was a bit much to take in.

Behind him, the CellPrint table had a long metal stand, on which hung some large see-through plastic bags hung from metal poles with tubes which resembled a larger version of the drip bag that gave him antibiotics when he was at the hospital that time after coming off his bike. Zac soon came to the assumption that this was what the Professor was trying to explain to him in the video. It was like he was laid on a large 3d printer, and his DNA was printed out of the weird goo. A jar next to it marked fibre was almost empty.

He examined himself. Everything seemed to be okay. He could hear and see, and smell, and even touched his face to see if this was real.

The door opened, and out came a man approximately 50 years old. He was wearing a lab coat, which had lots of pens in the pockets, and an ID badge dangling around his neck on a metal chain. He swept what was left of his hair across the top of his head and looked carefully at Zac.

"Hello again," he said.

Zac looked puzzled. "Have we met?".

"Yes, a couple of times now, but that doesn't matter. How are you?"

"Are you ... Professor Eric Mullins?" Asked the traveller.

"The very same," he said, "and this is my niece Rhea".

Behind him, there was a young lady about twenty years old. She was also wearing a white lab coat, but the bleached white was broken up by the flowing red hair parted in the middle, falling over her ears, and covering her shoulders. The paleness of her face was accompanied by the freckles on her cheeks.

Rhea gave a little wave and in a soft voice asked "How many times is it this time?".

Zac looked at them both, completely dumbstruck.

"We appreciate this must be difficult for you, we are still getting our heads around it too. To be honest, it still makes my brain itch trying to work out how this is even possible". Eric swept his combover back into place again.

Rhea looked carefully at Zac. He looked back at her. "You're going to think this is weird... but did it work? Did I time travel?"

The Professor nodded and cupped his hand around his chin in thought.

"Yes, it did," replied Rhea with an excited tone in her voice. "Welcome to 2008. What date have you come from?"

"17th February 2038," Zac replied, and he paused to think of something intelligent to ask, "What's going on, in this decade?"

The Professor smiled. "Good. It's the same as last time, that upgrade to the time circuits helped."

"Last time? But I don't remember doing this before. I think I would have remembered that!"

Zac listened as the Professor explained how tricky time travel was, and that it was even trickier to get to the destination accurately. From time to time Rhea would pop in some snippets of info, to break it down into simpler terms for Zac. Zac was grateful for this, because it helped, as Eric was very technical in his language and used lots of words that Zac didn't fully understand.

"So you know why I am here then?" Asked Zac.

"Of course. You're going to need this." She handed him a digital camera. "Take as many photos as you can, the more the better." replied the young assistant.

"We've modified it, so that every time you take a picture, it will auto-upload to the Lab, and I can put together a profile of the investigation.

"Is there a way to get there, without having to go through the caves?" Zac asked the Holoprof.

"There is a way. You need to go out of the Abbey, through the town, behind the cinema, and down the back fence, then head towards the river, and up Appleton Hill to get to Newhaven."

Rhea showed him the way to the main exit, passing him a coat.

"Here, it's cold out there". She said with a smile.

The outside was chilly and dark, and he zipped up the coat, pulling the hood up to keep himself warm.

It was difficult to get his bearings at first. He thought he recognised where he was but quickly became confused.

CHAPTER 13

Walking along the road gave him a euphoric feeling. It hadn't looked like this since he was little, and old memories came flooding back.

Scanning the area, he remembered the flickering street-lamp that never worked properly, which his dad constantly complained to the town council about.

He relived the fun he would have with his friend at Benny's house, and how they would swap their toys and fish at the river together, then walked past the shop where he used to go with his dad every Sunday, then noticed the bus stop he used to stand at, waiting for the bus to Charles Cramer High.

Everything was just as he had remembered it.

It was then that he came across the old side-cutting that lead down to his house, and the view of the dam. Zac was overcome with emotion, as he stared at the Dam in all its glory, completely intact, and full to the brim with water.

Was this a dream? Had it worked? Had he gone back to the past?

He remembered the dam, and how he had seen the wall

break, spewing its contents over the entire town, consuming everything in its wake, and he shuddered from the thought.

Flicking the latch on the gate, he opened it. It still creaked, the same way it did when he was younger, and he could remember the voice of his mum as she always used to ask his dad to "fix that damn gate".

He never got around to it.

The spring-powered gate closed with a resounding clunk, and his footsteps crunched up the gravel pathway towards the front door.

A moment later, he was banging on the brass knocker. The door opened, and his mum just stood there in front of him.

Tears started to well in his eyes, and he sniffed, trying not to cry.

"Yes," she said, expecting him to answer.

"I am..." he paused

She watched him as he stood there, not knowing where to look.

"Look, I haven't got all day," she said impatiently.

"I wonder if you...."

He stopped, remembering how much he hated her for killing everyone in the town, including his father, even though she hadn't done it yet. He loved her and missed her very much. Zac wondered if there was something he could do to stop it from happening.

"If you've come here to sell me something, I'm not interested," she replied, starting to close the door.

He looked at the floor, apologised and walked off down the pathway to the gate. This was going to be more difficult than he had imagined.

At the end of the pathway, he turned right, and disappeared behind the hedge, walking straight into his father.

His dad looked at him and stopped, staring. Zac stared too, and after a moment of stares, a whole silent conversation passed between them as they stood in the street.

"Do I know you?" asked Mike.

"Uh, no, I just have one of those faces."

"Are you sure?"

"I would know if we had met before."

Of course, Zac knew his father, but would Mike recognise Zac? After all, he was 30 years older right now, and his facial features had morphed into those of a 40-year-old man.

"What were you talking about with my wife?"

At that moment, the door opened, and Zac ducked behind the hedge for cover as she came out.

Zac put his hand in his pocket and poked the material with his finger.

Mike stared at Zac. "Is that a gun?"

"What do you think? I know you were in the military, so no funny stuff. Get over there, and stay behind the hedge," he beckoned with his finger gun, making sure there was enough room between them both.

Mike crouched, biding his time, weighing up all the options.

"You won't get away with this you know!"

"Shut up, or there will be consequences" Zac threatened, with a nudge of his finger gun.

They watched as the door opened, and his mother walked outside, shortly followed by a woman.

His mum got into the car, and the woman jumped into the back seat. The car started, and they drove off down the road.

"Okay, I don't know who you are, or what you want, but that's my wife, and I don't want you to hurt her."

"I'm not here to hurt her, Mike," said Zac.

"I'm from the government, sent to protect you from her, and bring her in for questioning."

"What? Why? What did she do?"

"I can't talk about it now, but what I can say is… You need to stay here, and I have to go after her."

"Stuff that, I'm coming with you," replied Mike.

"Okay, but no sudden moves. Understand?" said Zac. "Now, let's get that car from the garage, and go after her."

Mike walked out from behind the hedge, and up towards the house. He opened the garage door, removed the tarpaulin, and jumped into the driver's seat.

"Are you coming?"

Zac got in as Mike started the engine.

He reversed the car down the driveway, the garage door auto-closing, and put his foot on the accelerator.

The tyres squealed, and the car shot off down the road with a jolt. With the wind in their hair, Zac remembered how much fun it was, being in his dad's convertible, and was taking in all the scenery, in a blur, but he also knew that all of this would soon be gone.

What could he do to fix it? How was his mother innocent? Who was that woman? Lots of questions went through his head.

In the distance, Zac could see the station wagon.

"There she is," said Mike.

"Keep our speed steady, we don't want to spook her. We need to know where she is going."

"What did she do?" Asked Mike.

"It's classified,"

"But she is my wife. Hey man, I signed the official secrets act. I did my service. Tell me," Mike said, slowing down.

"Why are you slowing down?" Asked Zac

"Are you kidding me? She's my wife, I don't want her going to jail."

"I'm not supposed to tell you this, but she's a material witness in a major incident, and the woman in the car with her, is the prime suspect. We have to stay back and not be spotted, for your wife's safety."

"Well, why didn't you just say so?"

In reality, Zac didn't have a clue who the woman was but was quite proud of the story he had just told his father to get him on his side.

Mike put his foot down on the pedal, and the car sped forwards through the traffic.

Moments later, the main road forked right, and Rebeccas' car turned off the main road towards the dam.

"What are they doing? That doesn't go anywhere, except to the dam. They will spot us easily if we follow them. I have an idea."

Mike slowed down, deliberately missing the turning, and drove passed the side of the reservoir.

About a mile down the road, at the opposite end of the reservoir, he pulled the vehicle over into a secluded spot, hiding the car underneath some trees.

"Here, try these," said Mike, pulling a pair of binoculars out of the glove box.

Looking across the vast expanse of water, Zac adjusted the focus dial and could see the car driving up to the security booth at the entrance of the dam.

Rebecca got out and walked up to the guard.

He could see them talking, and then, quite by surprise, he pulled out his gun and pointed it at her.

The window of the car wound down, and an arm extended. There was a brief flash, and the security guard flinched as if he had been shot.

Zac expected the guard to fall on the floor, but something strange happened instead, and Zac was surprised when the guard walked into the security booth.

The barrier to the reservoir opened, and the car drove through.

Zac couldn't believe his eyes. *What on earth was going on?*

His mum's car went closer to the edge of the water, Rebecca got out, and grabbing a bag, walked onto the dam's gantry, overlooking the town.

She got halfway along the gantry, and stopped in an almost mechanical movement, standing for a moment, motionless. Then something peculiar happened, and Rebecca turned 90 degrees on the spot and climbed down the ladder from the gantry towards the water specimen collection zone.

Zac remembered seeing videos about this at school. This was the part of the dam where scientists and health officials would regularly check the water to ensure its safety for drinking and public use.

As she climbed down the ladder, with the rucksack on her back, he couldn't help wondering how he was supposed to stop this.

She reached the bottom of the ladder and pulled off the backpack.

Zac and Mike watched her put the rucksack onto the gangway. She opened it and reached inside with both hands.

Hoisting up the specimen retrieval chain, Rebecca attached the backpack and lowered it into the water.

In a moment of panic, he realised what was going on. The package was a bomb, and his mother had just planted it!

But what he couldn't understand was; what had made his mum, the nicest person on the planet, turn into a terrorist. This explosion would be the worst thing that this town had seen, and the biggest atrocity that would rock the entire country, uniting future generations against terrorism. Little wonder she was convicted and put into a chemical coma to serve her sentence.

Who was the woman in the back of the car, perhaps she had something to do with this. She probably did, she had to... his mum isn't like this; it had to be that woman... but she was in the car, and nowhere near his mum... this was all so confusing.

"What is she doing?" Asked Mike.

"She's planting a bomb."

"You're joking?" said Mike in disbelief, looking Zac straight in the eye," that'll kill everyone in the town, we've got to stop her,"

"That's why I'm here," said Zac trying to reassure his father.

"But you said she was a witness? Yet, here she is, about to blow up the dam," completely stunned by his wife's actions.

"I'm from the government, we lie for a living," replied Zac, pleased that his father now knew the truth about Rebecca.

Mike got out of the car and gave Zac the keys.

"What are you doing?" Asked Zac.

"I'm going to warn my brother, he's the local cop. And with my army connections, I will get them to fly in some troops and stop this."

Zac got out, "Is it okay if I keep these?" He asked, holding up the binoculars.

"Yes, have them." he said, "you've got to stop her, I'm going to my brother's house, he only lives up the road."

Mike walked through the hedge and headed across the field towards his brother's house.

Zac racked his brain. He was usually very good at figuring things out, but at the moment, he was a little stuck.

What should he do?

Zac considered his options carefully.

Call out to his mother? It sounded like a good idea, except, she wouldn't hear him.

Drive to the dam and disarm the bomb.

Yes, that would be the best idea, and even if he couldn't disarm it, at least he could remove it from the water and drive it to a safe place.

So, that was the plan.

Rain spattered on his face, and he wound up the window. Zac chucked the binoculars onto the passenger seat and pressed the button to put the convertible's roof up.

He looked at the car's controls, this was not like the cars he usually drove. It had an engine, a stick, and no AI to drive it. The closest to this was the arcade games he used to drive as a child.

The car started, and he put the stick into drive, then

pushed his foot to the floor, and it all came back to him. It was just like he was driving the cop car in 'Car Crazy 2' all over again.

The back wheels squealed, the steering wheel grabbed his hands, and Zac tried desperately to turn a corner. Grabbing the steering wheel with both hands, he gained control, as he let his foot off the pedal. The machine responded.

It didn't take him too much time to learn how to drive the automatic. Learning to avoid the other cars was a little more awkward, but the traffic was slow, so he had fewer problems than expected.

He could still see his mum climbing up the ladder to get back up to the gantry, as the convertible arrived at the turnoff towards the dam.

CHAPTER 14

By the time Zac arrived at the dam, he could see his mother getting back into the car and heading down the road towards the town.

What was she doing? Why was she doing it?

Those things would have to wait for now; first, he had to get rid of that bomb.

She narrowly missed a few cars while getting back into the main road, and other vehicles honked their horns to show their disapproval, as she continued into the town.

Meanwhile, Zac had escaped the traffic jam and was now driving up the road with the speedometer showing 80 miles per hour. He flicked the lights on to see better and put the windscreen wipers up to full speed to bat off as much of the rain as possible.

As he approached the guard's hut, he slowed down, spraying gravel everywhere as the car braked. Zac got out of the car and ran to the guard.

"Are you okay?"

"Yes, I just can't seem to move."

"I'm here to help," replied Zac "But I have to get that bomb first, and then I will come back for you."

Zac ran to the gantry, the rain completely soaking him.

He climbed down the ladder and looked around for the chain. Grabbing it, he pulled with all his might, but nothing happened.

On the wall was a mechanical winch. With both hands, he turned the handle. It clicked as the chain tightened, and Zac started to pull the backpack up through the water heaving a sigh of relief as the backpack broke through the surface, and then he pulled at it to swing it onto the gantry.

The backpack was easy to open with just a quick flick of a buckle, and Zac spotted the device beeping inside the plastic liner. He peeled the sides of the backpack away to get a better look and saw the bomb was quite large. There was a big lump of explosive which looked like a block of plasticine, and Zac recognised it as C4, from old movies, and some holoshows he had seen. There were some wires and a large red clock. It was counting down, and Zac panicked when he saw it flick from seven minutes to six minutes and fifty-nine seconds.

She must have only set a ten-minute timer.

Zac took a large breath, trying to relax.

He looked around and spotted a safe place to put it. There was a field, the perfect spot. It was less than a minute's walk from where he was.

Flapping the cover closed on the backpack, he tried to pick it up to put it on his back.

It wouldn't budge. The bag was chained to the winch, and onto the chain was a large padlock. Zac hunted through the pockets for a key, or something to pick the lock with, then realised how much of a stupid idea that probably was.

He padded his own pockets, wondering if he had something that would help.

Nothing, he thought, starting to give up hope.

Less than six minutes remained. He could try to defuse it, like the hero in the films he watched, but he didn't have pliers, or a screwdriver, and to be honest, he didn't have any training either.

His mother had made sure this bomb was going nowhere. The timer was slowly counting down, only 5 minutes left now. Rapidly running out of ideas, he watched as the timer flicked down to 4 minutes left.

This was it, and he knew whatever happened, he was running out of time... only three minutes and thirty seconds left before the bomb was going to explode.

Carefully, he unwrapped the bomb completely, and held it in his hand, with the chain and bag hanging from the keyring looped into a hole in the circuit board.

The plan? Turn the device upside down and put it into the water to fry the circuit. Easy peasy, right?

Nervously, he tilted the c4 and clock combo 45 degrees. He paused for a moment. This was going well, and with 3 minutes left, he was confident it could be done.

What mattered were all the lives he would save, including his father.

Two minutes, forty-five seconds, and he had now rotated it 90 degrees. Another pause, and a deep breath to calm himself.

With only 90 degrees left, and over 2 and a half minutes, this would be over in no time. It almost seemed easy, too easy. For a bomber to have chained the device inside the backpack, tied it into the bag with a keyring, and the bioplastic bag, they had certainly taken all precautions, but Zac knew he was smarter.

Rotating the bomb, he nearly jumped out of his skin when a buzzer went off.

Panicked, he turned it the right way up and looked at the clock. It was still going, oh yes, it was going faster, and faster, double rate, then quadruple rate. In less than a minute, he would be toast. He dropped the bomb onto the gantry and climbed the ladder to the main wall, then sprinted to the guard's booth.

His heart was thumping, his legs going, his arms trying to keep up, his lungs aching trying to grab as much oxygen as possible, he made it.

BOOM!

CHAPTER 15

Water pushed upwards, and the shockwave caused the air to vibrate with so much force that Zac was thrown from the blast, and his ears muffled as he hit the floor with a resounding thud. He lay there, completely drenched from the spray of water thrown everywhere from the explosion. After making a mental check of himself, Zac jumped into the car, still dazed. His only thought was to head to town and warn everyone what had just happened.

His ears still ringing from the explosion, Zac started the car, and put it into drive, then sped down the road towards the town. The speedo hit 30, 60, then 100, and the engine growled as the scenery blurred either side of him. The roof of the car became unclipped, ripped off with the wind, and flew off onto the road behind him.

As he reached the town, his hearing had almost returned to normal, and he braked with a resounding screech.

In the supermarket car park, Zac saw the strangest thing. His mother was just sitting in her car, staring at the dam. It was as if she was just waiting for it to explode. He got out, walked to her car, and knocked on the window. She didn't even flinch, just sitting there, staring at the dam.

Looking through the car window, various clues told a different story.

The car keys were in the ignition, her knuckles were white as she gripped the steering wheel, and she didn't move a muscle, her eyes peeled to the window. He opened the door and checked her pulse.

It was feint, but she had one. Putting his ear up to her mouth, he could feel her breath against his face.

"You've got to wake up" he shouted. There was no response. Above his head, Zac heard a helicopter flying into the town, and he spotted the Channel 14 news network logo as it hovered close to the fire station. There was another bang, and the ground shook. He looked up and saw a crack in the dam.

Grabbing the seatbelt, he unclipped it, and it snapped upwards, almost catching him in the face as it recoiled into the holder.

Someone wanted to make this look like an accident if she was ever found when the dam released its full force, but who? The woman? Who was she? Questions flew around his head.

More helicopters flew over 3, 4, no 5 choppers in all. They hovered above the other end of the parking lot, and he watched as soldiers expertly slid down the ropes onto the tarmac of the car park.

A man wearing camouflaged gear ran towards the car.

"You've got to get that car out of here." said the soldier.

"I can't move her," replied Zac

"Ma'am, we've got to go. I need you to move over to the passenger seat."

To Zac's surprise, Rebecca let go of the steering wheel and got into the opposite side of the vehicle.

"Get in, we have another huey coming in, and we need to make space for it," said the soldier to Zac.

Zac saw some buses coming down the road, heading towards the fire station.

With Zac in the back of the car, and his mum slumped in the passenger seat, the soldier twisted the keys in the ignition, and drove the car out of the supermarket car park towards the fire station, and the waiting coaches.

"Ma'am, you need to get out of the car and get on that bus, it will take you to safety." said the soldier pointing to where the buses were stopping.

"Sir, you need to get on that bus too."

The Soldier spoke to the driver while Zac and another passenger helped his mother onto the bus.

After she was sitting in the back seat, Zac got up and told the driver he needed to get off.

"Nope, no one's getting off buddy," said the driver in a determined tone.

"But I… *need* to go," said Zac crossing his legs.

"Okay, but I am leaving in two minutes," replied the driver.

Zac got off, and the driver stuck a thumbs up at the soldier who was guiding people on.

He sauntered down the side of the bus towards the other side, and amidst all the confusion, Zac sneaked away from the bus, towards his home street, hoping that his father would be there.

Above him was another helicopter, blades blowing dust and leaves everywhere, and a squeal from a speaker, then an announcement.

"This is the Army, You are being evacuated. Please proceed to the coaches in Burn street, outside the fire station. This is NOT a drill."

As people heard the announcement, they emerged from their houses. It repeated through the speaker, and some soldiers started running down the street, knocking on doors.

"You need to get to the bus," said one soldier.

"This is an evacuation, grab your medications, then proceed to the bus," said another.

People ran towards the bus, and an enormous crowd headed towards Zac.

He waded through the oncoming sea of people as fast as possible, as people were pushing and shoving against him to flee to safety.

The crowd of people thinned out as they went one direction, and he went the other, and Zac arrived at his old house.

"Dad?" He called out.

"Mike, are you here?"

There was silence. He looked around and remembered that his dad had gone to his uncle's house, on the other side of the lake.

That blast must have caused more damage than I realised, he said to himself, suspecting he might have a concussion.

Wondering how he would get there; he remembered his father's bike in the garage.

Rummaging around, he found his father's bicycle, and some old paintings that his mother and father had never gotten around to putting up, then cycled down the street.

The street was almost empty now, with only a couple of soldiers trying to entice people to leave their homes, and Zac could hear gunshots in the distance, with lots of shouting.

Another rumble from the dam and the news crew in the helicopter moved closer to take in more footage of what was going on.

Zac looked up. The line was more like a large crack now, and water was spewing out, with large chunks of debris and brick being flung by the force of the water. This was going to go, and there was no stopping it.

There was another loud bang, this time it was coming from the area where Zac had been with the coaches, and he spotted a soldier with his rifle in the air, trying to break up a riot in the crowd.

The noise of the crowd quietened, and Zac looked over-head, as three of the helicopters headed off back to the army base.

He looked back at the crowd and watched as a woman was arrested, and then the crowd of people separated into lines and people were escorted onto the buses.

The first bus started on the journey out of the town, and Zac watched as it headed towards Appleton Hill. Zac continued cycling through the street, peddling as hard as he could towards the dam.

More water and bricks gushed out and exploded from the wall, and Zac knew he was running out of time. He peddled harder, as hard as he could to get up the road, and by now water was dribbling down the road in small streams. He got off the bike and ran uphill towards the turnoff to the guard's booth.

———

People in the town were now dropping their belongings, rushing, and running. They pushed and ran towards the coaches and their chance of survival. This was no longer an organised crowd of evacuees, but more like a crazed mob, pushing as far and as hard as they could. More shots rang out, this time from the soldiers down in the town. An army man shouted. He raised his weapon and aimed at the mob and shouted some more, waving his rifle to direct people into the coach. The crowds piled onto the coaches as fast as they could.

The doors closed on the second coach, and it soon started its journey uphill towards the police roadblock. Another coach followed behind it.

Rebecca was glad to be on coach number two, happy that they were on their way. She shifted her gaze to the dam and watched in horror as water spewed out and smashed into the houses below.

The third and fourth coaches filled quickly. A man started chucking wads of cash into the air, and as people's greed got the better of them, he climbed onto the bus, as the doors were closed, and the fifth coach was on its way towards Appleton Hill.

———

By the time he had reached the guard's booth, the guard had gone, and the ground shook, as large chunks of the wall finally gave way, and were spat outwards by the force of the water, to the waiting town below.

The water followed.

This was no gush, this was a deluge, a tsunami, and in seconds a million tonnes of water left the dam. There was nothing he could do, as Zac watched as the level on the side just dropped. Turning around, he saw the torrent of water throwing itself into the town.

Zac remembered what was going to happen. He had seen this all before, as he watched it on the TV at school. He knew some coaches wouldn't make it, and that the one his mother was on barely got to the top of the hill.

The helicopters in the air were trying to fly away, and they were being buffeted by the sheer force of the wave. As the water level dropped, so did the air pressure, grabbing an army helicopter, and sucking it into the dam.

Amidst all the chaos, a beautiful rainbow shone its colours across the town.

At the edge of the dam, the ground near Zac gave way, and in seconds he was sucked underneath. Behind him, what was left of the guard's hut bobbed up and down in the mud soup. He struggled to breathe with the pressure against his chest, trying to look for something to grab onto.

The next thing he knew, he was being flung at a massive

velocity, out of the gap, and into the town. He saw cars, houses, people, trees, and so much water.

It was the best that he could do to stay above the surface, and several times Zac went underneath again, then bobbed back up.

In front of him, another tree which he narrowly missed, and an entire row of houses. Then, he spotted it... his house, a speck in the distance, becoming bigger and bigger by the second. There was no way he was going to avoid this.

His body slammed against the building, the sound of water covered the sound of the windows smashing, and there was nothing he could do. His head hit the brickwork, and everything went black.

Zac's unconscious body, bruised and battered, stayed there for a moment, and as the water subsided, it slid underneath the water.

CHAPTER 16

2 038

Inside the Lab, a rotating emergency beacon flashed, and a buzzer sounded.

A robotic woman's voice spoke through the overhead speaker "Historical change occurred" it said.

Zac sat up on the TripleScan table and put his feet on the floor.

He stared at the Holoprof and asked, "What on earth does that mean?".

"History has changed" replied the Holoprof.

"How? I've not been anywhere, and I've only been laid on the table for ten minutes."

"Ten Minutes for you, but it could have been an entire lifetime for your time clone." Replied the Professor.

"When Latimer copies you and sends you back in time, you wouldn't notice anything different. But in reality, the time clone that arrives in a different time and space can make plenty of changes." Replied the Professor.

"What are the changes?" Asked Zac.

"I have compared the original version of history retrieved

from your brain and actual events, and there have been the following changes."

"1. Rebecca Drummond is no longer in jail."

"2. Records show that Rebecca Drummond was never considered a suspect in the dam bombing, instead, video footage of a man fitting your description was issued, and an arrest warrant was declared one month after the flood. The warrant was overturned because historical records show that your body was found, and drowned. A victim of the flood."

"What? I died?"

The rectangle showed a news broadcast with video footage of Zac on the gantry handling the bomb. The footage was blurry, and the wanted poster and description sounded nothing like him.

"That's ridiculous. I tried to stop that thing going off, and they think I planted it?" asked Zac in utter disbelief.

"I have compared the data, and that photo-fit looks nothing like you."

"Does it say what happened to my Dad?" Asked Zac.

"The only data pertaining to the whereabouts of Michael Dean Drummond is that he was never found, presumed dead when the dam collapsed, along with over 10,000 other people." Said the Holoprof.

"I have got to find him," replied Zac.

"You said, I can break the rules, does this mean I can go back again?"

"Of course. Just be aware that although *you* may meet yourself, and that will be okay for you, other people may become confused, if they see you both together, and that will get you noticed. Don't forget your main mission, you have to destroy Latimer"

Half listening, and not taking much in, Zac's stomach grumbled. "Got it. I'm starving. Have you got anything to eat?".

"There is a vending machine in my office" replied the

hologram pointing towards the computer suite, just kick the bottom of the machine.

Zac walked across to the computer room, gave the machine a swift kick and the door popped open. He grabbed a fizzy drink, a tin of rice pudding, some saltisnax and a berrypop bar, then sat in the computer chair and ate.

While he ate, he sat there wondering how he could have made such a difference if all he had done was laid on a table and pressed a button.

"While you are eating, allow me to show you what happened to your time clone". The Holoprof's video window appeared, and Zac watched as hundreds of data windows cascaded in the air. There were photos and video recordings, CCTV footage, internet articles, and more. The Professor then converted all the findings into a simulated video to show Zac what happened.

Zac watched with enthusiasm, taking it all in as he scoffed the saltisnax.

———

Approximately one and a half hours went by, and the video ended, Zac's eyes were getting very heavy, and he was yawning, just to keep himself awake.

"My sensors show you are tired," said the Professor. "There are some blankets in the specimen room, in a trunk. Please help yourself to one."

Zac grabbed a blanket, went into the computer suite, and adjusted the office chair to a laid-down position. "Is there any heating in here?".

"Of course, and I can lower the lights if you would like."

The lights lowered, and Zac soon fell to sleep.

CHAPTER 17

Zac woke up and looked at the computer. 8:38 am. He kicked off the blanket and raided the vending machine for some breakfast.

"Hey Professor. I need to speak to mum, do you have an address for her at *this* time?" Asked Zac.

"Good Morning Zac. Records show she lives at 42 Gibcliff Crescent, Newhaven," replied the Holoprof.

Zac walked to the main door of the lab, through a decontamination airlock, and away from the glass doors. The crypt looked strange, not quite what he had expected, and as he walked away from the glassy white box of the laboratory, his heels clicked on the stone steps as he slowly walked up towards the cloisters.

Looking around, he remembered that this was where his family used to go for Sunday mass. It was so different now, and it seemed smaller and darker. The doors were the same though, big oak arches of wood that creaked when he opened them. It was still dark outside, and he looked at his watch. It hadn't been long since he had travelled in time, but it didn't seem like anything had happened. Even watching the video he still couldn't believe his eyes. The woman, the bomb, the water, his mum.

He turned left, walked through the streets, then a right turn, passing the cinema and onto the fence, eventually reaching his mum's house.

He knocked on the door and pressed the bell. From the inside of the house, Zac heard footsteps clomping on the floor, getting louder and louder as she got closer. The light flickered on, illuminating the porch door. It opened, and a woman stood in a dressing gown and walking boots.

Without hesitation, she grabbed him for a hug.

"Zac, it's good to see you."

Completely taken by surprise, he didn't know what to do. He settled after a second and hugged her back. This was one of those mum-and-son hugs he hadn't had in such a long time. Emotions overtook him, and his eyes welled up with tears.

"Hi mum" he whispered.

"Well, don't just stand there, come inside for a cuppa". He looked around at the place. The fittings and decorations were meagre and drab, with none of the mod cons that Zac's apartment had, but it had electricity, and actual windows and anything was better than his mum being in a coma prison for a crime she didn't commit.

He noticed the old sofa they used to have when he was growing up, a little more worn now, but still looked good. Even the old rocking chair he used to sit on when he was a child was there, and it rocked gently as he sat on it. While he waited, he took in the atmosphere, remembering some things in his life, associated with some items in the living room.

Rebecca came out with a teapot and poured steaming tea into two cups, plopping two sugar cubes into one, and a dot of milk in the other for Zac.

"What brings you here, sweetheart?" She asked.

"I just missed you and thought you might like the

company" replied Zac, trying desperately to sound like it was a regular thing, and nothing compared to the fact that he was just glad to see his mum for the first time in over 30 years.

"But you only saw me yesterday, and twice in a week is a pleasant surprise. I have some washing up that needs to be done. Could you come and help?".

"Sure," Zac smiled and grabbed a tea towel.

She filled the washing-up bowl with water, and some 'washbar' washing-up soap, grabbing the dishes and putting them into the water.

"Mum, I don't understand why you don't get yourself a sonowasher."

"I don't want one of those newfangled things, they are too tricky to use," she replied.

"But Mum, it would save all of this," said Zac putting away the plates.

"All of what? Me washing the dishes and drying them? Next, you will say I don't need a washing machine, and not be allowed to be breathing fresh air, and go into the back garden for some exercise, you're right, I don't need any of that," she said in a sarcastic tone.

"Besides, I can't afford one."

"I could get you one, Mum."

"I know sweetheart, you offer every time you come round. It's almost as if you don't want to get involved in doing something together." She looked at him with a caring smile, putting another plate onto the draining board.

"I know you mean well sweetheart, but honestly, I am happy with the way things are."

"Okay mum, but the offer is there if you ever change your mind."

"If your father were here, it would be just as much washing up, his shirts on the line, I would iron his trousers, and his underpants..."

"Mum! Way too much information," said Zac, embarrassed.

She stopped for a moment and teared up. He put the tea towel down on the sideboard, walked towards her, and put his arms around her, giving her a reassuring hug.

"I still miss him love."

"I know mum, I know. I'm here," he said reassuringly.

Whilst Zac's actions had released his mum from coma prison, his father was still gone.

They stood there for a moment in silence, with a gentle breeze wafting the smell of fresh bacon and eggs from one of the neighbour's houses down the street.

"That's enough of that now, let's put this stuff away, and I will rustle you up something to eat."

"Okay, mum."

She cooked up some eggs, with a bit of the ham hock she had left over from yesterday, and they sat down at the table to eat omelette together.

"Mum, do you remember much about that day?" He asked.

"That was such a long time ago, but I will never forget what happened. It was your birthday, you came downstairs, and your face lit up when you got your present. It was that notebook you had always wanted. I drove you to school, and then went home, and then I answered the door…"

She paused.

"And then…" she pondered, stuck on what to say next.

"I don't quite remember all of what happened, but I know I woke up on a bus. Someone told me that a nice young man helped me. It must have been one of those soldiers who were dealing with the evacuation."

"I looked out of the back window of the bus, and I will never forget seeing the coaches behind us being washed away by the water. All the people looked terrified."

"Did they ever find out what happened to dad?" Asked Zac

"It's funny you should ask, I was only telling your brother last week what happened, and we managed to piece more events together." She paused for a moment and took a breath.

"Your Uncle Graham told me a while back, your dad turned up at his house on the day of the breach, ranting and raving about a bomb. We think he had seen the bomber planting the device and tried to stop him."

Zac held a smirk inside, as he realised how skewed the facts were, and that his mum had got the idea that the bomber was a man.

"Graham gave him the keys to his jeep, he headed towards town, and that was the last he ever saw your dad."

"The rubbish part is, we never even found his body, but there were so many people taken that day and washed out to sea." She paused, gazing out of the window for a moment, then returned to the conversation.

"The peas are cooked. Would you like some with your ham?"

"Yes please, pile them on."

There were so many more questions to be answered. He had to know.

They spent the day together, Zac helping his mother with the chores, and carried on chatting about how everything was going, then ended up on the couch together watching his mum's favourite TV show The Amnesty.

Zac fell asleep on the couch. Rebecca draped a blanket over him, and then went to bed.

CHAPTER 18

By the time his mother got out of bed, Zac had already been up for a couple of hours and was getting ready to leave, to make his way back to the lab.

He wanted answers, and the only way he could get them was to ask the Professor.

Zac and his mother ate breakfast together. He said goodbye and headed off to find the answers he so desperately wanted.

———

The security camera scanned Zac's face, and the door opened with a hiss, like the sound of a slow steam valve, and Zac entered the airlock.

Seconds later he was in the main lab, and the light switched on, illuminating the entire room.

"Holoprof on," he said.

"Hello again Zac," replied the hologram as it appeared in front of him.

"I need to look for Dad, what information do you have on him?"

"Accessing files," said the Professor pausing as it scanned the data retrieval system.

"Michael David Drummond, brother of Graham William Drummond, born to Janet and Bernard on…"

"Stop!" Zac said, interrupting the hologram.

"What about the Heyworth security guard?" said Zac curiously. "He was nowhere near the town when the dam collapsed."

"Records show that Oliver Black survived and currently lives at 68 Monell Drive."

"Does he know anything about dad?" Asked Zac quizzically, happy that he had got some information from the Holoprof.

"Sorry, that information is unavailable."

"Yea, yea, I know," said Zac sarcastically.

He went through the Holoprof's menu system, and no matter how hard he tried, he couldn't find any data for events that happened after his father had visited his brother.

Frustrated, he tried a fresh set of questions.

"Professor, bring up the camera footage from the dam. I want to know more information on the woman who was in mum's car."

"Searching" came the reply.

After a second or two, the Professor showed a video window, with a list containing clips, named and dated.

"Show me that one" Zac pointed at the 3rd one down with his finger. The video played.

Inside the rectangle, Zac could see his mum's car approaching. The car stopped, and she got out. All of this seemed exactly as he remembered it so far.

The guard tapped on the window. There was a flash, and seconds later he was walking back to the booth and opening the barrier.

"Rewind to the flash," said Zac to the Professor.

The video skipped back and paused a couple of seconds before the flash.

"And… play" Again the video flashed.

"Rewind and slow that down please," Zac said with a curious look on his face.

"Of course" replied the Professor as the video rewound.

There was a flash, and even after slowing it down, pausing it, zooming in, and taking out shadows, which seemed to make it worst, Zac was still clueless about what the flash was for, or whether it was even relevant.

"What about the woman in the back of the car?" Asked Zac.

"I have no data to suggest there was a woman," replied the Professor.

"So who is that?" Zac pointed at a figure in the back seat, trying to dodge the cameras.

The Professor did some video magic and sharpened and define the image.

"Who is she?" Zac asked, screwing up his eyes, trying to get a better look.

He had so many questions, and he had to find her.

"Okay… Play the rest of the video,"

The video played, and Zac watched as the clone Zac was seen from the News helicopter trying to defuse the bomb.

He watched as his mum's car was driven back into the town, and the woman got out.

"Freeze-frame" Zac shouted at the Professor.

The image of the woman was clear, and they could both see that this was not the suspect's real face.

"The mask she is wearing is obscuring facial recognition," said the Professor.

"I have to go back."

"If you wish," said the Professor, closing the video window.

"If she knows what happened to my mother, she probably knows what happened to my father."

He lay down on the table.

"I'm ready to go again, Professor."

CHAPTER 19

Zac opened his eyes. He was back in the lab again wearing the same starchy-feeling clothes, very stiff and not very comfortable. Recalling the video footage of the first time he had travelled, he looked around to see if he was in the same place. On the CellPrint table were a torch, some food, and a note.

Zac.
    Please use these supplies to help you on your quest.
    Rhea.

He got up, grabbed the torch from the table, put on the boots and coat, and walked outside into the night.

Heading towards his Uncle's house, Zac noticed that the dam was full and the wall completely intact.

Zac considered all of this. The water was still here. There was still time to stop this. He walked up to his Uncle's door and pressed the doorbell.

"I'm coming, I'm coming! Jeez, can't a guy just have one

day off without interruptions?" He shouted in a thick Scottish accent as he clomped his way to the front door.

A man approximately 40 years of age, about five foot ten, of heavy build, with scruffy white hair, stubble-faced, wearing a pair of dungarees opened the door.

"What do yer want?" He asked.

Memories flooded Zac's mind of his aunt and uncle. His aunt, the farmer at Appleton farm, her pigs, the camping trips in the fields during childhood summers, and his uncle, the big strapping guy, a police officer who no one in the town messed with.

"Who are yer, and what do yer want?".

"er... I'm from the government, and I'm looking for my... my... Mike Drummond, have you seen him?" Asked Zac.

He turned his head and shouted into the house. "Hey Lucy, there's a guy here from the government looking for Mike. Have you seen him?

"He was here earlier, and went to the town, to meet up with his wife."

"Thanks for that," said Zac, feeling a little more upbeat, that he had some sort of lead.

"He left his phone here." Said Graham passing him the device. "When you find him, can you make sure he has it"?

"Sure," Zac put the phone in his pocket.

The two men went quiet, and they had come to the end of their conversation.

"So I'll be going then," said Zac taking his foot off the doorstep, as he backed away from the man.

"Thanks for dropping by, and I am sorry I couldn't help you anymore," said Graham.

"Thanks for your help." Said Zac, waving as he walked down the pathway.

The old man went back inside, closing the door after himself.

Zac turned around and walked down the pathway.

He made his way into the town, fiddling with the phone as he walked.

He switched it on and typed in his dad's birthday as the password. Even though Mike had been in the army, he was still pretty predictable like that.

The screen turned on, and Zac looked through the call history, calendar, photos, and contacts to see if he could find any more clues.

Arriving at his old house, he experienced more memories and more questions than before.

Zac knocked on the front door. There was no reply. He snuck around the back of the house and crept in through the toilet window, away from prying eyes.

The inside of the house was dark, and he cupped his hand on the torch to prevent the beam from being seen from the street through the windows.

In his father's study, he found some documents referencing the Professor, and took photos of them with the camera on his dad's phone.

He was leaving by the front door of the house when he saw the headlights of a car coming up the street.

The car stopped, and Zac hid in the shadows.

Two men got out, one was tall, the other short and tubby.

"The uncle said he was back," said the tall man with an upper-class English accent.

"Yea, well he ain't here now, is he?" Replied the smaller man lighting a cigarette.

"We have to find him, or it's our heads on the chopping block" The small man motioned with his hand across his neck, pretending to slit his own throat with a finger.

"I don't get what he wants with the man, what's so special about him anyway?" As he spoke, smoke escaped from his mouth, and Zac noticed that the smaller man had a London accent.

"I don't ask questions, I just get the job done, and get paid." said the tall man.

"Yea, yea, so what are you buying this time? Another boat?"

"A yacht, it's called a yacht… honestly, you are so uncultured it beggars belief sometimes."

"We need to keep looking then, or no yacht for you, and no plasma telly for me," replied the short man as he got back into the car.

"We can't see in this light anyway, let's do this in the morning." Replied the tall man as he closed the car door.

Who are they looking for? Zac wondered to himself.

He grabbed the phone and took a photo of the car as it drove off. The phone's flash lit up, and Zac dropped it on the floor in surprise.

The car stopped, and the fat man got out.

"What was that flash?".

"I think you are seeing things," replied the tall man.

"Nah man, I know I saw it." He walked towards the house. "I saw you, you can't hide."

As he walked into the house, he pulled on the door. The little that was left of it broke off its hinges and clattered onto the floor. Zac's heart thumped as the man stepped into the doorway. There was a crunch as the man's boots trod onto some glass, and Zac put his hand over his mouth to stifle any breathing noises he might be making. This was a terrible mistake because the dust on his hand made his nose very sensitive, and Zac noticed that familiar feeling of a sneeze starting to tickle the top of his nose.

Peering through the shadows, he could see that the short man was holding a gun. His heart beat faster, and his hands became clammy. The hairs on the back of his neck stood on end, and he stepped back slightly to get further into the shadows. As he moved back, he felt something touch his shoulder, and Zac froze.

The fat man ventured further into the house, he'd pulled out his mobile phone and was using it as a torch. The feeble beam was not worth bothering with, and he switched it off, then slid the phone back into his pocket.

The tall man poked his head in from the front door and shouted, "Did you find anything?".

"Nope."

"We are needed back at the cinema."

"Whatever, this is a waste of time anyway". The fat man turned and headed towards the doorway. Zac breathed a sigh of relief, relaxed a bit, and his shoulder fell backwards, not far, but enough to knock against the wall, hitting him in the shoulder blade with the handle of the grandfather clock in the hallway. There was a small click, and a whir as the gears of the clock kicked into life, a couple of ticks, and silence.

The fat man hadn't heard a thing, and he was just going out the front door when there was a loud dong from right behind Zac.

The man turned around just as the clock struck again, pulled out his gun, and fired it in Zac's direction.

Bullets whizzed by Zac's head, and he ran towards the fat man to overcome him. This was his fight-or-flight response, and he wasn't in the mood to fly. The clock struck again, and this time the tall man came inside to see what all the commotion was about.

Zac, his head just out of the shadows, was running straight for the man, and with no plan, just wanted to stop himself from being shot.

The man pulled the trigger. Zac's chest felt warm, and he collapsed backwards onto the floor, blood trickling from his chest onto the lino. The clock struck for the fourth time.

He looked upwards as the man pointed the gun straight at him.

There were some flashes and two loud bangs, and the man left. Zac's eyes closed, and everything went black.

CHAPTER 20

2 038

Zac's eyes opened.

"Historical event occurred." Said the Professor.

"Another one?" Replied Zac cluelessly "I was only on the table for a few minutes."

He paused in disbelief, still taking in how this worked, then resumed. "Okay, can you display the video please?"

The Professor collated all the data from vehicle cameras, news reports, people's photographs, and reports that had been submitted to the court files as evidence, then showed it all as one video.

He watched as the two men drove away, then saw the flash from his dad's phone.

He thought for a moment, then came up with an idea.

"Can you do something to the video to show the number plate?" Asked Zac.

"The video quality is too low. I have already added the best filters and resolution possible to clean up the image," replied the Professor helpfully.

"I searched for information on any online accounts and found the data that was on your father's phone."

"Excellent, check the GPS coordinates, this will help us find where he went."

"Sorry Zac, but that data is not available, because your father's phone didn't have GPS on it."

"What else have we got?" Asked Zac.

"34 photos, 71 contacts and 152 calendar entries were found in the phone of Mike Drummond."

"Show the pictures," said Zac eagerly.

All the photos popped up in a fashion that resembled someone taking lots of instant photos and then throwing them in a pile on a table. Each picture slid to a space on the screen and Zac could see all the images. He looked carefully, spotting images of him and his mum, then the photo his clone had taken, of the back of the car before it drove away.

"There, that one," he pointed at the picture. "Can you blow that up?"

"Of course" replied the Professor. The photograph showed full screen and automatically brightened.

"That's it, and can you zoom in on the number plate and give it a bit more contrast?"

The Professor extrapolated the numbers and letters on the number plate, and a separate window opened, scanning through the driver's database. Moments later, there was a beep, and the screen started flashing.

"The vehicle belongs to Thomas Collins, also known as fat Tommy. He has no known address and is believed to be living in his car, according to police reports. He is associated with a tall man who we have no further data."

"So that's why he needs the money. Can you get an ID on the other guy?".

"Sorry, there is not enough information in the picture to find a valid ID."

Zac got up off the table and went to the vending machine for some more food and a drink.

When he came back, the Professor was playing and

rewinding the video and collating information to update his database.

He watched as more information was revealed about the last jump back to find his dad, and cringed in horror as he noticed the video ended with a newspaper clipping that showed the bomber was found dead, and that justice was served.

Zac pondered this for a moment, then realised what he had seen.

"My clone died... again!"

"That's the beauty of clones" replied the Professor "If they die, you are still alive. But that doesn't mean that you have to mourn the loss. On the positive side, they think you're dead, so whatever happens now will be a surprise if you decide to go back."

"Hmm, good point," said Zac "It would help to find out who they are, and why they are looking for me."

Zac and the Professor talked more, and they pieced together more information about what was going on.

"There's only one thing for it, I must ask Tommy. Find his car, and let's start the machine up Professor."

CHAPTER 21

2 028

Zac looked up, and it took him a moment to get accustomed to the light. A man was looking down at him. He was stocky, wearing a guard's uniform, and there was a brass badge on his left breast pocket with the name Bob Stafford on it.

"Okay Fella, take it easy now. I'm going to get you a blanket, and then I'm going to get some help. You stay here and rest."

Zac struggled to move, weak and exhausted, and his chest hurt. Moments later Bob came back with a blanket, and laid it on top of Zac, tucking it in.

"Just stay there, I won't be long". He pulled his mobile phone out of his pocket, typed in a number, and then left the room.

Zac waited for a while, and as his eyes grew accustomed to the dark, he spotted he was still in the lab.

Had something gone wrong? Why did the lab look the same? Who was the security guard? Was he the guy with the spotlight from that time when he first found the lab and climbed down the well? There were so many questions. He had to get out of here.

Inside the lab, an orange beacon was flashing, and the lights were off.

He pulled himself up, took the blanket off, and noticed that he had nothing covering his arms. Looking down, he was completely naked.

He turned around and looked for the fibre jar. There wasn't even one there, just a large-sized DNA goo jar that was half full.

Zac sat up and his eyes started to focus properly. He waved his arms around to activate the lights.

Nothing happened. This was very confusing.

Why weren't the lights working? Where were his clothes?

As he pondered the answers to these questions, he heard a crash of thunder, followed by some footsteps. The footsteps were quite close now, and doors were opening and closing.

He could now hear two distinct sets of feet, and a woman talking to someone.

Would they come in here? Should he hide? Who were they?

Fearing it may be the woman who was in the back of the car, he needed to get out of there. He stepped off the table, into something sticky, then fell over and banged his head. The door opened, and Zac, dazed and confused, watched as a torch beam flickered around the room.

From the shadows, Zac saw the stocky security guard and a woman with long hair, wearing a lab coat.

"He was here, I swear. He was dead. I gave him CPR and brought him back." said the guard, flicking his torch around.

"Well, he's not here now Bull," said the woman with a softer, more relaxed voice.

"I'll go to the generator room, and you stay here, and lock the doors."

He switched on his spare walkie-talkie and passed it to her.

"Once I get there, I will let you know, and you can walk me through the reset procedure. Just press this and talk."

"I have a PhD in physics, I'm pretty sure I can use a walkie-talkie." She said smiling at Bull.

"Of course Miss" He gave a thumbs up and walked out of the room.

A few minutes passed, and a crackle came over Rheas' walkie-talkie.

"I'm at the generator. Are you there?"

Rhea pressed the button on the microphone and spoke into it.

"Yes Bull." Replied Rhea sitting on the chair next to the computer.

"Okay, what do I do?"

"You need to start by unlocking the cage door."

A moment passed, and the speaker clicked again.

"Done. What now?"

"Good, now you need to look at the front of the three-phase unit. There should be two banks of panels in front of you. You need to switch off all the switches."

"Done."

"Now starting from the top, switch on the two master switches at the same time."

"Okay, doing it now."

"Now switch on the left bank of switches first from top to bottom."

"All done, do I do the same with the right switches too?".

"Yes, from top to bottom," replied Rhea.

As Bull flicked the switches, the capacitor room hummed, the security system activated, and the computers all booted up.

Rhea tapped on a few keys, and the security cameras came online.

Within seconds, banks of lights lit up the crypt hallway to the lab, and the lights flickered into life in the laboratory.

She walked into the Lab and looked straight at Zac.

Like a frightened rabbit staring into headlights, he stared straight at her, not moving. The woman before him was approximately 5 foot 6, wearing black-rimmed glasses, a lab coat, and black trousers.

The embroidery label on her lab coat said R. Manebeck - Lab Assistant.

He tried to get to his feet but was too weak.

He looked into her eyes, her red hair parted in a fringe at the front, and some wisps hung on either side, while the rest was swept back into the long plait he had seen earlier. Her perfect nose and freckles showed off the prettiest blue eyes.

"Are you okay?" She asked softly, offering him a hand to get up.

Zac sighed and stuck out his arm.

As he got up, she realised his nakedness, and took off her lab coat, wrapping it around him, revealing her pink blouse, and black trousers underneath.

"My name is Rhea, what's your name?"

"It's me, Zac." He said in disbelief. *Had she forgotten who he was?*

"Do you know where you are?" She replied.

"Infinity Labs."

"And how did you get here?"

"In the machine" he replied, curious why she was asking.

Rhea paused for a moment and then helped him up to sit on the table.

"What do you mean?... from the machine?" She asked with a confused look on her face.

"I came to the lab, and the Professor helped me to come here... can you tell me what the date is?" He asked.

"Let me get this right, you know the Professor? Do you know me? and you know this lab? and-"

"I travelled in time" he replied, interrupting her.

Sensing a potential threat, Rhea calmly walked over to the table, and with her back to Zac picked something up.

"Please put your arm out."

Zac obliged, and Rhea took out a syringe and stuck him with it. Within seconds, he collapsed, and she grabbed a specimen trolley from the specimen room.

She could hear Bob's footsteps getting louder, and quickly bundled Zac onto the trolley, then wheeled it skilfully into the specimen room, covering him with a sheet.

As Bob Stafford came into the Lab, Rhea had already returned to the computer room and was typing on the keyboard, as if nothing had happened.

"Thanks, Bull, I just need to set up a few diagnostics, and then we can go back home."

"This is where I saw him," he said, pointing at the sticky substance on the floor.

"Strange, I have seen no one." replied the Professor's assistant.

"Is there anything else we need to do here, Rhea?" He asked.

"Not really, I just need to set up a few checks. You can go back to your post. I'll call you if I need anything."

"Okay, I will just do one last sweep on my way out."

The lab door closed, and Rhea could hear Bob whistling as he walked along the corridor, checking each room as he went.

Without hesitation, Rhea picked up the phone on the desk and pressed quick-dial button number 1.

"Uncle Eric, you've got to get down here, something incredible has happened."

"What's happened? Are you okay?".

"I can't talk about it on the phone, just get down here fast."

She put the phone down.

CHAPTER 22

The airlock opened, and in walked the Professor. His blue plastic overshoe protection crinkled against the laboratory floor. He entered the computer room and inserted his keycard into the console.

"Hey Rhea," he said as they hugged.

"Hi, Uncle Eric." She replied.

"Okay, tell me what happened."

"Bob found a man on the CellPrint table, who claims to have travelled in time."

"What have you done with Bob?" asked the Professor.

"Just told him to go back to his post. We don't have to worry about him, he's covered under the official secrets act," replied Rhea.

"You did the right thing. Bob doesn't have the clearance for that sort of thing. If we give him a bottle of his favourite whiskey, he will be content with that."

"Where is he now, this time traveller?" asked Eric with a look of excitement on his face.

"I put him in the specimen room, he's sedated for the moment."

"Okay, let's see what happened," he said, as he accessed

the security controls. They watched as he rebound the footage and pressed play. The Professor turned the dial to speed up the playback, and they watched the experiment from the previous evening unfold. How Rhea had put the pig onto the table, the duplication, and how the pig hadn't lasted for long before its cellular cohesion gave out, and ovine DNA ended up all over the floor. On the screen, he saw both himself and his assistant leave the room as they went home for the night.

The image on the monitor changed erratically from the everyday look of the white room to being plunged into darkness as the storm knocked out the electricity, and the generator kicked in. Then it went dark again with only the flashing of the orange beacon. Eric changed the playback speed once more, and they watched with awe and wonder as the monitor flashed, and the CellPrint kicked into action. They both stared in fascination at the monitor, and layer by layer, the CellPrint knitted DNA cells together at breakneck speed.

"What the... It's not supposed to go that speed?" Said Rhea in utter disbelief. She put her hand out to slow down the video.

"Let it go... I want to see what happens" replied the Professor rubbing his hands with excitement.

The Professor watched with enthusiasm as layer by layer; the machine constructed something from the DNA goo. Arms, legs, organs, head, chest, and face became recognisable. The final layers were added, as the tip of Zac's nose, chest and kneecaps were complete. Needles inserted themselves into the brain, and a glow came from the capacitor room as his brain scan was uploaded. Blood was introduced, the needles retracted, and the body jerked on the table as electricity was pumped into it. The lights switched off, and everything went silent.

A moment later, light from the main corridor poured into the dark, and Bob Stafford could be seen entering the room on the monitor. The Professor's excitement rose as Bob performed CPR and brought Zac back to life.

A big grin broadened across the Professor's face.

"This makes no sense. He said he came from the future... but how?" Asked Rhea.

"I need to examine him."

Rhea left the computer suite and disappeared into the specimen room.

She returned with Zac, laid on the trolley, and Eric went through to the main lab to help her lift him onto the Triple-Scan table.

"Pass me the adrenaline dear," he asked Rhea while checking for a pulse and trying to get a vein. After swabbing the area, he injected the needle into the vein and pushed the plunger.

He waved some smelling salts under Zac's nose, and Zac quickly came around.

"I have so many questions," said the Professor.

"It's you! You are younger... and real," Replied Zac.

They chatted, and the Professor learned that this wasn't Zac's first trip in time, the Professor making notes as they talked. The conversation veered this way and that.

They talked about Zac waking up in the lab several times. Fascinated, the Professor carried on making notes, and he included a mention of fibre.

"This is all very fascinating, but I need to know something," said Eric.

"Why are you here?" Asked Rhea.

"Precisely... Why *are* you here"? Asked the Professor scratching his head.

"I need to find a man called Thomas Collins, he may tell me what happened to my father." Said, Zac.

"I remember your father, it's a shame what happened to him," replied the scientist. "I don't know a man called Thomas Collins though."

"I remember a man of that name, he used to work in a corner shop, down the road from where I lived. They got raided for selling counterfeit cigarettes and he went to jail. He was a short guy, and spoke with a London accent," replied Rhea.

"That's him" replied Zac.

She walked over to the computer and tapped on the keyboard. Entering his name in the search engine, she found him almost straight away on a dating website. He had even added an address online.

"Before you go, I need to do some more tests," said the Professor. He took Zac's Blood pressure, did a brain scan, and took a swab to test DNA. The professor concluded his findings and approved Zac fit enough to go outside, with Rhea as a chaperone, of course.

"Make sure you take as many photos and recordings as possible so that we can match the evidence together in the future," said the Professor.

Moments later, the old man grabbed some spare clothes from the car and brought them through for Zac.

Zac got dressed, and the Professor and Rhea chatted for a while, discussing the dangers of going to find fat Tommy.

She reassured her uncle that the karate lessons he made her take when she was younger had proven useful sometimes and that he didn't need to worry, as two of them versus one fat man would be okay.

Happy to leave them to it, the Professor bid them both good night and went home.

Zac finished putting his shoes on, Rhea slid on her coat, switched off the lights, and they both exited through the airlock.

Walking up the stairs with someone else was a pleasant feeling, and he was glad he was no longer alone in this weird past.

At the top of the stairs, they walked across the flagstone

flooring of the Abbey through the big arched doors and out of the building, through the graveyard, and towards the car park.

With Rhea in the driving seat, and Zac in the back underneath a blanket, the car started up, and Rhea drove the car down the road towards the rising roadblock and the security hut.

"Evening Bull" said Rhea as she pulled up, showing him her security pass.

The big man leant down towards the car, peering inside. His military frame towered over the car, with his tight shirt still struggling to fit, even though it was an extra large.

Every time they met, she was reminded of the stories he used to tell her when she would walk to the lab from school, and wait in the booth for her Uncle to come and pick her up. Stories about how his friends used to call him Staffy, because it was a type of bulldog, packed with muscles built for strength, and that was Bob all over.

Except for Rhea.

Caring for her when she was little while she waited to be collected from the booth meant he had become fond of her, and very protective… the bigger brother she never had. He had even taught her some karate moves that her old dojo hadn't, so she could protect herself when he wasn't around.

"Evening Miss" he replied, looking around.

"Everything alright now? Did you find that man?"

"Yes, all is good, I think you scared him off. Uncle Eric came to help me look for him and check on the computers to make sure he hadn't stolen anything, but everything is okay, and we haven't seen him since."

"I will keep an eye out, and double the watch, just in case, and I will let you know if I see him," he replied swiping her card. "All good for now Miss, see you tomorrow."

"Goodnight Bull". She drove off.

CHAPTER 23

Zac pulled off the blanket, sat up, and clipped his seatbelt in.

After about 15 minutes, they arrived at Tommy's house in a downtrodden part of the town, and the car came to a stop.

Rhea switched off the engine and lights, got out of the car, and then peered through the driver's side window.

"Stay here," she said pointing her finger at him, like someone who was telling a dog to stay.

Zac did as he was told, and Rhea walked across the road, reached the front door, and then pressed the doorbell. The porch light switched on, and the silhouette of a large man stood behind the glass panel in the door. It opened and fat Tommy stood in front of Rhea.

"Oi, What's your game? Do you have any idea what the time is?" He shouted.

Zac couldn't hear what Rheas' response was, but it didn't seem to please him.

"Who the hell do you think you are?" Zac could hear Tommy shouting.

They chatted for a moment longer, then completely out of

the blue, Tommy raised his arm, and Zac could see he was holding a gun.

Rhea walked into the house. Tommy looked from left to right, to check no one had seen what was going on, and walked inside, closing the door.

A million thoughts went through Zacs' mind.

Was Rhea okay?

What had she said?

Why did he pull her inside the house?

What was he going to do with her?

What should Zac do now?

He scanned the front of the house. It was a large bungalow, with a neat garden, and the front door was next to the bay window. The lights were on, and Zac could see into the living room area.

Wondering what on earth was going on, and fearing for Rheas' life, Zac pondered on the situation for a brief moment. He watched, and he could see the man with his back against the front window inside the house.

There was only one thing for it. Without hesitation, he clambered from the back seat into the driver's seat and started the engine. The motor growled as he pressed the accelerator pedal, and he slipped it into drive. With a quick turn of the steering wheel, he was soon hurtling towards the house, without a single thought for himself. He just wanted to get in and get Rhea out.

The car's crumple zone obliterated the front door of the house, making the car six inches shorter. Glass sprayed through the air, as the mechanical beast contacted the front room windows, and the 2-ton chunk of propelling steel came to a halt. His ears ringing, he got out of the car and looked straight at Rhea.

She looked downwards at the hulking man, and his gun was next to him on the floor. Dazed and confused, the man didn't even move when Zac picked up the gun.

"Where is Mike Drummond?" Asked Zac, aiming the gun at Tommy's head.

"What the hell? You're dead! I killed you," said Tommy, trembling.

"Well, now, I'm back, and I have a score to settle," said Zac with a menacing look on his face.

"Why would I tell you?" Replied the man, getting to his knees.

"FREEZE!" Shouted Zac. "Don't move any further, or else."

"Or else what?" Said Tommy, calling his bluff.

With a slow and deliberate movement, Zac pulled back the hammer on the pistol. The man stopped.

"You wouldn't," said the man, standing on his feet.

"He would!" replied Rhea, "look what he did to my car, and your house."

Zac moved the pistol to the right and squeezed the trigger. Plaster filled the air as the bullet hit the wall and smoke emptied from the barrel of the gun. He re-centred the sights of the pistol on the man's head.

Tommy leant back on his knees, and went quiet, dread filling him as fast as the colour drained out of his face. He raised his arms, surrendering.

"You wouldn't shoot an unarmed man, would you?" He asked with a look of fear.

"Where is Mike Drummond?" Zac said firmly. "Answer me, or I *will* shoot."

Rhea stepped between both men, blocking Zac's shot, and facing Zac.

"What are you doing? You can't do this," she said, pleading with him.

Before Zac answered, Tommy, stepped up, and pointed the tip of a knife at Rheas' ribs, with his other arm around her neck.

"Put the gun down, or she gets it," he said, his London accent coming in really thick.

Zac, completely thrown by the whole situation, lowered the weapon. As he lowered his arm, he saw an opportunity and took it. With a squeeze of the trigger, the bullet entered the man's leg. Blood splashed all over the wall behind him, and Tommy, completely surprised, dropped the knife, and then fell backwards into a heap.

Rhea quickly jumped to the side, and Zac pointed the pistol at him.

"Where is my… my… Mike Drummond?" He shouted.

"You shot me… I can't believe you shot me! You're dead, and you shot me," said the man, holding his leg.

"And I will do it again if you don't tell me where he is."

"Okay, okay. I don't get paid enough for this… he's at the old cinema, in the basement."

"You buried him in the basement?" What the….?" Zac fired another shot, this time at the floor, close to Tommy's good leg.

"Buried?" interrupted Tommy, "the tough old sod is still alive… he lived through the flood!". He said it in an almost admirable tone.

"We need to get there, but the car's a wreck," Asked Rhea.

"Give me your car keys?" Zac waved the gun at Tommy.

"Here," he made a feeble attempt to toss them across what was left of the living room. They landed at Zac's feet, and he scooped them up, then headed towards the front door.

"Phone?" Demanded Rhea, with her arm outstretched.

"It *was* on the coffee table until you drove into the house" he grunted. She looked around and picked it up off the floor, then shoved it into her pocket.

"Okay, let's go, he's not going anywhere," Zac said, looking at Rhea. She moved closer to Tommy and tore off one of his sleeves.

"What the?"

Rhea wrapped the tourniquet around his leg.

"Hold it like this," she said, showing him how to twist it, to stem the blood loss.

Zac and Rhea left the house and got into Tommy's scruffy yellow hatchback.

CHAPTER 24

Zac got into the driving seat. He looked at the gearstick and didn't have a clue.

"Here, you do the driving, I need a rest," he said, trying to hide the fact he couldn't drive a car with a manual gearbox.

Driving down the street of twisted metal posts, houses damaged by the floods, and complete isolation, the car picked up every bump in the road. Around every corner, he remembered little snippets of his childhood. The vacant space where there had once been a wooden youth group hut, was now replaced with only electric wires sticking out of the ground, and a bent-over basketball hoop. The mesh wire fence hadn't even been strong enough to take the strength of the water from the dam, and what remained was some rusted mangled wire in a heap on the floor.

The houses were all but demolished, and those that hadn't been smashed to smithereens by the force of the water coming at a hundred thousand litres per minute had been destroyed instead by the family car, a caravan, or delivery trucks.

He could see the tidemarks of the water on the sides of the buildings and remembered watching the tv at school. The disbelief when he and the other children watched it all unfurl. How the looks on their faces changed from delight at watching a disaster movie, to a sinking feeling as they all realised this was their hometown, and these were members of their families and friends, fighting for their lives to scramble onto the coaches.

These feelings had been kept hidden for so long, but now, they built something up inside him, and as everything around him became a blur, he spent a moment in quiet and shed a tear. *His father must be here somewhere,* he thought, as they arrived at the cinema.

"I can't go any further," she said, pointing at the fallen mobile phone mast, and rubble "we have to ditch the car here".

They pulled up. He wiped his face and got out of the car. He was so driven by the want to find his father that he started to run from the car through the cinema car park.

"Oi, wait for me," shouted Rhea as she ran after him, her lab coat flapping in the wind, and wisps of red hair being blown in her face.

He looked back and slowed down, waiting for her to catch up.

Walking across the car park, through the rubble, and twisted metal, they chatted about the rescue back at the house and forming some sort of plan to find his father. She would go upstairs into the gallery of the cinema, as Zac wasn't good with heights, and he would check the basement, and then they would check the ground floor together.

As they passed the ticket booth, they walked in through the big black doors.

There were posters, disposable cups and cartons littered all over the floor, and Rhea noticed that someone had made a pathway through all the rubbish and debris.

"Someone has been here," she remarked to Zac.

Meanwhile, Zac was reliving old memories of the cinema

with its sweet smell of popcorn, the ice cream and drinks servers in stripy pink and white tops and black trousers, holding trays at their waists with straps hung around their necks.

"Mint choc chip," he said out loud.

"What?" Replied Rhea confused.

"Nothing," his face flushed.

"I'm off upstairs, see you in ten minutes back down here."

He gave a thumbs-up and opened the door to the basement.

As she climbed the stairs, she passed a long window that looked out onto the car park and found the door to the upper circle.

The door creaked, and he stepped down the concrete steps, each one echoing his footsteps in the darkness. *If anyone was down here,* he thought, *they would hear him coming a mile off.*

He slowed down, carefully placing the toe of each shoe onto the ground first, to minimise any sound from his shoes.

His heart was beating fast, and he was struggling to listen as blood pumped through his head and his ears. His head pounding, he slowed his breathing to heighten his senses, and calm himself.

———

The view from the upper circle was just what Rhea had expected from the posters in the lobby, and although it was darker, there was still a sense of grandeur and atmosphere.

She hunted up and down the aisles, not sure what to look for. There wasn't enough room to hide a person here. Perhaps Mike was dead and just dumped on the floor some-where. She looked up and down the rows of flipped red velvet chairs. From the rail, she could see the stage clearly, with its trapdoors, a remnant from the days when the organist used to rise through the stage playing the organ as the trolley people served their ice creams, popcorn and drinks.

All around her, there were wrappers and cartons, a reminder of how everyone had just got up and left all their rubbish behind them and evacuated the town before the big wave hit.

———

The basement was musty, and Zac suspected it probably hadn't even been aired in a long time, let alone seen the light of day. This seemed pointless, and he doubted Tommy was telling the truth about his father being here.

He wrestled with that doubt, and it got stronger and stronger as he looked behind the wine cellar shelves, and through boxes of theatre clothing discarded from the old days before the building was modernised and turned into a cinema.

There was not a lot of anything, nothing useful at all. No clues, nothing that could link Tommy to this place, or the tall man, or his father. His face grew angry "This is a waste of time" he said to himself as he climbed the stairs.

———

Rhea passed the window on the way down, and waited in the lobby, looking at her watch. At that moment, the bell rang on the main door. It swung open, and there was a dark figure in the hallway.

CHAPTER 25

Tommy stared at Rhea. She looked back at him, and the tall man entered behind him.

"Gotcha," he said, his thick London accent filling the air with menace.

Taken aback by the re-emergence of fat Tommy, she stepped backwards. The tall man entered the building. His neat appearance didn't compare to Tommy's, and Rhea wondered why they would even hang out together.

He was wearing a black, full-length trench coat, which covered a dark blue suit and waistcoat, white shirt and tie. The man was clean-shaven except for a neatly trimmed moustache with tiny curls at the end. His shiny black Italian leather shoes radiated wealth and an upper-class upbringing, making him a very sophisticated-looking gent. His eyes and full head of hair made him look a lot younger than the moustache would allow him to be.

"Where is your friend? The one who ruined my holiday home," Asked the man pulling out a gold pocket watch from his waistcoat pocket, and then checking the time.

Rhea stood, stunned, not knowing what to say. She stared at the basement door.

"I... I don't know" she said, turning her gaze to the tall man, trying not to give Zac's location away.

"I haven't got all day, tell me, or there will be... consequences". He snapped the clasp shut on his gold pocket watch and put it back into his waistcoat, then reached into his trench coat and pulled out a weird-looking weapon that looked like some sort of stun gun.

At that moment, the basement door opened, and all three looked straight at Zac, who was taken completely by surprise.

"Get over here" urged the tall man, waving the weird gun at him.

"I thought you said you killed him," he said to the fat man.

Tommy's face tightened up in anger. "I.. I... I did, but he's back, and he tried to kill me."

"I wasn't trying to kill you, I was just trying to stop you from shooting her," he said, looking at Rhea. Zac walked across the lobby towards her, thoughts racing. The plan to find his father was far from his mind, and the safety of the lab assistant, who had now become a good friend, was on his list of top priorities right now.

Tommy pulled his revolver from his jacket pocket and pointed it at Zac.

"Can I shoot them now?" He asked. Zac said nothing, and Rheas' face dropped.

"Put it away Tommy, I've got other plans for these two," said the tall man.

The tall man aimed the weird gun at Zac and pulled the trigger. The gun made a quiet noise, and Zac felt something hit him in the chest. What followed was something he didn't quite expect.

He looked down, expecting to see blood. There was nothing there.

"Ha! You missed" he said mockingly.

The tall man stayed quiet for a moment with a smile growing on his face, then he shot Rhea as well.

In the moments that followed, some strange things happened. The place where he had been shot became warm, and Zac felt something he couldn't explain.

"What did you do to me?" He asked.

The tall man put his fingers to his mouth, "Stop talking please." Zac tried to open his lips to speak, and although the words were there, and his mouth was moving, nothing happened. He panicked, and decided to make a run for it, grabbing Rhea's arm, then headed for the front door.

"Stop running and stay exactly where you are," the tall man commanded.

Both Rhea and Zac involuntarily stopped running, and just remained glued to the spot.

"You're probably wondering what's happening right now." The tall man commented.

"That's got 'em stumped," said Tommy.

Zac and Rhea just stood there.

"These are Nano bullets. From the moment they hit you, they navigate through your clothing, skin, arteries and veins, and they control your nerves, muscle, auditory, and brain functions. You are both now completely under my control."

"Voice-controlled morons," said the fat man with a big grin on his face. "You both have to do whatever he tells you to."

"Walk through that door," said the tall man, as he waved the gun. Realising they had no choice, and with involuntary actions, Rhea and Zac reluctantly walked through the Staff Only door and headed down a narrow corridor to the room at the end.

"Hurry, we ain't got all day," Tommy said, limping behind them, blood dripping from his leg.

The door of the office opened, and they both noticed the smell of cigar smoke in the air. There was an empty chair in the left corner, and a large table in the middle of the room.

Behind the table sat Zac's father, in an executive leather chair, with a large cigar in his mouth.

"Good job on catching them," he said, looking at both men. Mike Drummond stood up from his chair, puffed on his cigar, and blew out a large plume of smoke.

He looked at them as they entered the office. Zac looked back at him, memories flooding back from his childhood, but none of them was about the man in front of him. His father was kind and loving. Someone who liked to wear a t-shirt and jeans, a non-smoker. This man, however, was mean-looking with a cigar and henchmen. Zac remembered how his father was always *at the office* but never said much about his work. He was really surprised that his dad could pull off this other life, without any of them knowing, back at the family home.

Zac looked at the table. It was covered in blueprints of the dam.

"Answer the boss's questions." Said the tall man.

"Allow me to introduce myself. My name is Michael Drummond, these are Fat Tommy, and Colby Spencer-Hall, my associates."

"Now, who are you?" He asked, looking at Rhea.

"I'm Sharon Gillespie, and this is…." She paused. "My cousin Brad."

Tommy looked straight at Zac and pointed.

"He's the guy I killed."

"That guy drove into my house," said Colby.

"He tried to kill me" Tommy glared at Zac.

"And I gave you that tourniquet," replied Rhea.

"Is that true?" Asked Mike.

"Yes, but he had just grabbed Rhea and-," Zac stopped, realising his mistake in saying Rhea's name. Tommy looked at Rhea.

"I thought you said your name was Sharon," he said, with a menacing scowl.

"Rhea? Rhea Elizabeth Beckman, Erics' niece? I thought I recognised you," Mike said with a smile.

"You know my uncle?" She asked, dropping her guard.

Tommy looked straight at Mike.

"Boss, you know this girl?"

"It's been a while, but I met her uncle a few times, back in the day."

Colby turned his head to Zac. "So, cousin Brad... who are you?"

Zac stared at the table, blueprints of the dam, and a lump of C4 were enough evidence to prove to him who was really behind this, his Father... but why?

Remembering back to the lady from the PHPC, he picked out the first name he could think of.

"My name is Agent Santelle, and I'm from the government. I am here to take you all in for the bombing of the Heyworth Dam," he said with a cheeky smile.

"And where pray tell, is your gun and badge?" asked Colby.

"How the hell does the government know?" Asked Tommy to Colby.

"They don't, he's faking it. He doesn't even have a gun," snapped Colby. "Be a good chap and fetch something to tie these two up with."

A few minutes later, Tommy came back with some rope.

"Want me to do them, Boss?" Tommy asked Mike.

"Too messy," replied Mike "We should tie them up and let the flood take them."

Mike left the room, a cloud of cigar smoke following him, and Tommy put the chairs together, back to back, as Colby monitored Rhea and Zac, waving the gun now and then to remind them it was still in his hand.

Rhea was first. He ordered her to sit down, and her wrists were bound to the arms of the chair. While Tommy tied her legs to the chair legs, she kicked out at the man.

Tommy backed off, a bit shaken, and pulled the gun out of his pocket.

"Please try that again, I would love an excuse to shoot your little friend here."

Rhea looked up and froze. "No, please don't!" She cried in fear.

Zac walked over to the vacant chair and sat down. "Back to back, bound and gagged. This all seems a bit cliché" he said as Tommy tied their arms and legs together.

"I wouldn't worry about it, this is the easiest bit... wait until the dam bursts," he said with a smirk. "Then you'll get what's coming to you."

The men left, the door closed, and a key rattled in the lock.

Zac looked around him. Amidst the smoke, he couldn't see anything in the room that would help them. The only things in the room were the table, and chairs they were sitting on a picture on the wall of how the old cinema used to look like in the old days, and a bunch of rolled-up posters on the floor.

Zac, still under the influence of the Nano bullets, imagined scenarios where he somehow had super strength and could snap himself out of the ropes and then use the glass in the cinema picture to cut the ropes that held Rhea. He also considered the possibility that he could move the picture with his mind, willing it to fly off the wall, the glass magically cutting the ropes, freeing them both. Zac stared at the picture. He willed it to move. Nothing happened.

Wriggling behind him, Rhea had freed the gag from her mouth. "Are you okay?" She asked.

Zac, still trying to move the picture with his mind, broke his concentration, and tried to muster a reply, but a muffled urglegurgle just came out instead.

She moved her head to help, but they were both so tightly bound, she only succeeded in banging her head against his.

Zac gave a muffled ouch noise, and pulled his head away from hers, to prevent it from happening again.

"If you bend your head towards your chin, you might be able to loosen the strap around your mouth," she said.

He wriggled, and the gag gained enough space to slide down his face.

"Thanks" he replied. She looked around the room.

"Got any ideas now?"

He considered they both think about telekinetically moving the picture of the wall, but decided against it.

"Nothing comes to mind," he replied.

They went quiet for a moment, and Rhea asked, "What was it like? Time travel?"

"Er… there isn't much to tell. I lie down on the table in the lab and wake up moments later. It's a bit like going in a lift. You enter the lift on one floor, then exit on another floor, and everything has changed."

"But what about pain, or smells or…"

"Well, I get pain, because of the needles. I can smell bacon all the time, and I just don't understand why."

"The pain is because of the needles, and the bacon smell is because you are created from reconstituted ovine DNA."

"I'm what?" He asked with a confused look on his face.

"The process we use is to clone pigs, to help solve the food crisis," she replied, shifting herself on the seat to get comfortable. "But somehow you travelled from the future, and…"

"Wait, so you're saying I am made from pig DNA?" he said with a disgusted tone in his voice "No wonder I always smell bacon."

"Ovine DNA is the closest to human DNA, which is why we use it to grow organs for human transplants. You're the first whole human ever created, and somehow it happened using our machine." She tried to wriggle more, hoping it would loosen the ropes and help them escape.

"Try to twist to your left a bit," said Rhea.

He twisted, and the ropes tightened even more. "This isn't working".

"And to the right?" She suggested.

"I can't see that working either, but it's got to be better than telekinesis," he remarked.

"What?"

"Nothing,"

He wriggled, she wriggled, and the chairs wobbled.

In a moment of pure genius, he piped up, "I've got an idea, let's rock the chairs over, and hopefully they will smash against the floor."

She agreed, and they rocked the chairs, left to right, until they became off balance, and the chairs crashed to the ground, with Rhea and Zac banging their heads together.

"dammit, I bit my lip... I even taste the bacon," he commented.

The chairs, still in one piece, hadn't even cracked or splinted, holding their shape as they had done since they were built.

"So what do we do now brains?" she said sarcastically.

"How am I supposed to know, you're the one who works in a lab," he replied.

"But it was your bright idea," she replied.

"Arguing will not get us anywhere" he tugged on the rope, and the smell of bacon got stronger. Something smushed, and his chair jerked an inch lower to the floor.

"What are you doing?" Asked Rhea

"I'm trying to get us out of here, what do you think I'm..." His voice changed to a more gravelly tone, and he spit out some blood onto the floor.

"What is that?" He shouted in fear.

"How should I know?" She asked sarcastically. "I don't have eyes in the back of my head."

The chair lurched again, and Zac's head hit the floor with a squelching sound.

He tried to speak, but only a gurgle came out of his mouth. Rheas face felt a weird sensation of wetness, and she couldn't understand where it had come from.

"Have you...?" She started to ask but was interrupted by the stench of bacon now coming from behind her. There was a loud squelching sound, the ropes slackened, Zac's chair dropped to the floor, and Rhea was splashed by a viscous reddish-coloured fluid. The stench of bacon became prominent in such a way that it resembled the odour that a skunk would spray, and Rhea knew that this smell wasn't going away soon.

She wriggled free from the ropes and looked at the mess on the floor. Zac was nowhere to be seen, and all that remained were the chairs, rope and the ovine goo.

She grabbed the door handle and ran out of the door into the darkness.

CHAPTER 26

2 1 May 2038
Zac sat up and looked at the clock.
"Historical change..." the Professor started to say.
"I know, I know... historical change occurred," said Zac interrupting, irritated by the same old thing.

"Don't you have any other way of saying it?" He asked the hologram.

"I am programmable, you can help me be more human if you want to."

"Really? So, instead of saying historical change occurred, you could just say *Hi Zac, how are you doing? While you were asleep, some stuff happened in history that I think you would be interested in.*"

"Of course, would you like me to update my response?"

"Yea, that would be good, more... human, and less machine."

"But I am a machine" replied the hologram, flickering with a shimmer.

"So... what happened this time?" Zac asked.

The hologram stood back, and the rectangular video screen played the historical updates. Zac learnt how his past self, had met Rhea, and how they had gone to the cinema, the problems being captured, and then watched the video camera footage in disbelief as his body had melted onto the floor.

"What the...?" Zac watched in confusion, "What just happened?"

"Ah, I was going to tell you this bit," the hologram paused the video.

"But how could you, it's only just happened?"

"Because it's happened before, it's how we figured out that you had travelled from the future,"

"Wait, what?"

The Professor explained that, although this was the third time that Zac had travelled to the past, this was all out of chronological order.

"The first time you sat in the machine, was not the first time you arrived in the past."

"So, you're saying that I have only just gone back to the past now?"

"You've got it" replied the hologram.

Zac still didn't get it.

The video played, and the Holoprof stopped at the point where Colby was voice-controlling Rhea and Zac.

"That tech, it must be from the future," said the Professor.

"Why do you think that?" Asked Zac.

"Because I only started developing it last week."

The video screen fast-forwarded and played the scene of them falling over on the chairs, struggling to get out of the ropes, and him melting into a puddle of goo on the floor.

"Pause," instructed Zac, "Okay, so what happened?"

"You appear to have dissolved."

"Well, duh, I know that, but why?"

"Preliminary findings based on the analysis of the data we collected, confirm that your ovine DNA can't seem to sustain cohesion for over 240 minutes, and after that, it degrades on a molecular level."

"What does that mean in English?" Zac paced the room, taking it all in.

"Short version, you can't be a clone for longer than four hours."

Zac thought about this for a moment. "But I seem to have been okay the rest of the trips… why is this happening now?" He asked.

The Professor's rectangular video screen faded for a moment and shrunk to the top left corner. Another screen popped up, brighter than the first video screen, and showed a horizontal line.

The axis line showed three dates on the left in chronological order and the numbers 1 to 3 on the right-hand side of the axis line.

Small lines arced from the numbered markers to the date markers, and Zac could see they referenced the journeys he had taken.

"So, what you're saying is, you met me for the first time, even though it was the third journey I took?" he asked quizzically, trying to understand the timeline graph.

"Exactly," said the Professor with a smile on his face. "The first time we found you, was when we realised the potential of the machine. We hadn't intended it to transport matter through time, it was only meant to clone, and reproduce foods, etc for the growing population of the planet, but as soon as you came through, we had to hide our research, to prevent the military using it, for whatever destructive means they could have."

"So, I was an accident?" Zac looked at the Professor, trying to make sense of the whole thing.

"Travelling in time was simply not something we had expected" replied the Professor, trying to get Zac to understand him.

The time traveller took all this in.

"Going back to the pig DNA. I read you can grow human

DNA on pigs, like when they grew the ears on the back of rats, and stuff," Zac said, trying to sound sciencey, but suspected he probably wasn't quite up to the level of the Professor.

"Certainly, things have moved on from there though, and we have grown not just parts of humans, but experimented with cloning humans with an ovine base, to prevent the rejection issues which occur when different DNAs are introduced in the human form."

"So that humans don't reject the organs you create," said Zac.

"Exactly," confirmed the holoprof.

Zac's mind went wild, and he remembered watching weird science fiction programs when he was a child, about how clones were grown, and how the entire world would end up eventually looking like clones, no one reproduced, and we all looked the same.

He laughed to himself, wondering if the hologram was advanced enough that it might read his mind.

"The answer to your question is, we simply don't know why you melted, but what we can say is, that your molecular cohesion lasted for approximately four hours."

"So, you're saying that every time I go back, I only have four hours?" He said, quickly dismissing the idea of a cloned human world.

"Exactly that". The timeline window disappeared, and the video window re-emerged. "Would you like to carry on with the video?".

"Sure, why not… give me a moment though" He walked through to the food dispenser and grabbed a drink and some popcorn. "May as well make a thing of it".

"If you would like, I can stream the video to the monitors on the computer suite, and you can sit and watch it from there."

Zac sat in the swivel chair, munching popcorn, and

drinking another fizzy drink, whilst the Professor switched the video stream to the monitor.

He watched as events unfurled and pieced things together then looked at the Professor. "Thank goodness Rhea escaped".

Behind him, there was an empty whiteboard and a wipeable marker.

Zac brainstormed on the whiteboard, first with names of people, and then he added dates, and more and more information until it resembled a suspect list from the old detective show he used to love when he was a child. Flicking through the journal, he wrote some things down, putting question marks next to them, to show if there was any relevance, or if they would somehow make sense, but came to no conclusion.

He stood back from the board, picked up the popcorn, and popped some in his mouth. Examining the board he said "I just wish I understood this"

"What has my father got to do with this? How could he make me think, it's my mother's fault when it's his?"

"There are other possibilities," said the Professor through the computer's speakers.

"Such as?"

"Well... I would tell you, but it's easier to show you instead". The lip on the side of the whiteboard frame lit up, and a red laser beam scanned across the surface, picking up every detail of Zac's drawings.

Behind Zac, a computer made a beeping sound, and he spun around on the chair, dropping half of the popcorn on the floor, but looking in awe at the monitor as it displayed the contents of what he had drawn on the board, onto the display.

On the monitor next to it, there were pictures and articles, bits of sound clips, and more flashing, and Zac could tell that the Professor was searching for something. A few seconds later, on the first screen, the mind map that Zac had drawn, was pulled apart by the computer. People were put into categories, internet articles were added, and more information was extrapolated, and included on the screen.

Zac watched with excitement as each drawing slid from one part of the screen to another, like a jigsaw puzzle that was completing itself. It finished, and Zac studied it for a moment, then got off the chair and picked up the rest of the popcorn.

"This information is categorised with what we already knew, and what you have found out, as you've gone back into history. We know it wasn't your mother's fault the dam burst, and that she was wrongfully convicted."

"Okay," said Zac, taking it all in.

"And we know that your father…"

"What's that?" Zac pointed at the bubble underneath his father's name, which had a red circle with a padlock inside it.

"I don't have access to that file."

"But you're like a supercomputer, how can you not have access to that?"

"It's encrypted with government encryption, so there is some information, they don't want us to find out."

Zac finished the rest of his fizzy drink and tossed the can into the recycle bin.

"And those other items?" He asked, pointing at a few greyed-out sections on the screen.

"Those are queries that will make sense when we have more information," said the Professor.

"Right then… I need to go to the little boy's room before I go back and find out more."

CHAPTER 27

As Zac woke up, he looked around him and saw the familiar white ceiling of the lab, and he spotted the clock on the wall, with the date, and time on it.

Standing up, Zac checked himself all over and was pleased that this time, he had clothes. Next, he proceeded to the airlock, up the stairs to the main abbey and towards the big wooden doors.

He spotted the shafts of light coming through the stained glass windows and basked in the warmth for a moment. The door handle turned, and he pulled open the big heavy door onto the street.

The gentle breeze was warm against his cheeks, and he walked away from the back of the abbey, through the grave-yard, towards the car park, the gravel crunching, and the birds tweeting as he headed towards the cinema. He needed a plan but didn't know what it would be yet, or if anyone could help him, but he knew he needed to do this. Approaching the edge of the car park, he noticed a car and darted behind a tree.

The car pulled up into the car park, and he watched as Colby and Tommy got out. Colby walked into the abbey, and

Tommy limped down the pathway until he got to the door, then stayed outside, and lit up a cigarette. A phone rang, and Tommy opened a flip phone, then talked into it.

"Hello?"

"Yes, of course, it's me... who else would answer this number?"

"I'm at the Abbey with Colby, trying to find the assistant and that time traveller. Honestly, we've been everywhere, and all Colby does is order me around. Who does he think I am, his chauffeur or something? I'm ready for a break."

He paused for a moment, and his voice quietened. "Sorry, I didn't mean to shout Boss, but sometimes that guy winds me up. We will find them," he replied, stubbing out his cigarette.

He flipped his phone closed and put it back into his pocket, then breathed a sigh of relief, and lit another cigarette.

Zac waited for a little more. The abbey door opened and Colby walked out, closing the door behind him.

"All clear," he said.

"Where to now then?" Asked the tubby man.

"We need to check the reservoir,"

"Again? we already did that twice,"

"The Boss just texted me, and says we have to do it again," replied Colby.

"This is ridiculous... We were doing alright by ourselves, and then he comes along and ruins it all."

"We can't help it if a time traveller arrives from the future," replied Colby

"Not that guy, the new Boss... I mean seriously, we've been good together as a team, getting all this stuff organised, and now... he comes along and wants to take a cut of the action." He mimicked the voice of Zac's father "You have to do what I say, now that I'm the boss. Do this, do that, do the other... shine my shoes, make my lunch, seriously who does he think he is?"

Colby waited for him to finish and calmly said, "He's the guy you are going to replace".

Tommy relaxed and smiled "Yea when that dam goes, he's gonna be right in the middle of it, and once he's dead, I'm the boss."

"That's right, and I will be there to make sure it happens."

"But what do you get out of this?"

"I am just happy being the mayor of Newhaven, once this all plays out. The people will love a mayor like me". He adjusted his tie, and stood up straight, imagining the cheers and celebrations of the crowds as he becomes the man in office.

"But first, we are going to find that time machine, and the people who know how it works."

Colby and Tommy got into the car, and the car drove off.

Zac ran back to his house, to warn his father about the plan they had for him.

CHAPTER 28

Arriving at the family home didn't take long, as Zac had taken the shortcut across Edoc Moor behind their house. As a child, his parents had always warned him against taking the shortcut, citing incidents of people getting stuck in the bogs and quagmire. Thankfully, he was older and more experienced, and it had been dry enough to walk on. Running across the moor made things faster, and he made it back to his home in just under 15 minutes.

He knocked on the door, and his father answered.

"You!" He said in surprise as he opened the door.

"Yes, me! You realise you kidnapped a government agent!" Said Zac in an authoritative voice, to intimidate the man.

Inside his pocket, Zac pointed his finger and made it obvious he meant business.

Mike, seeing that Zac had a protrusion from his pocket, put his head outside, and looked to either side, scanning the street.

"Come on in," he said cautiously.

Zac walked inside, and behind him, his father quickly closed the door.

"Were you followed?" He whispered.

Zac, unsure of what was going on, kept up his agent persona and answered confidently.

"Me, followed? They would have to be good to get one over on me," he said reassuringly.

"I've come to talk you into helping me arrest Colby and Tommy, and I want you to give yourself up to."

Mike paused.

"Okay, you got me, man,". Mike held out his hands, wrists together, ready to be handcuffed.

As Zac put out his hand, he quickly and skilfully grabbed Zacs' wrist, pulled it towards him, and in seconds Zacs' entire world had turned upside down, and he was laid out on the floor, the wind knocked out of him.

Zac looked up, half dazed, to see Mike leaning over him.

"There's something I have to show you," he said, reaching for his pocket.

Fearing that Mike was going to produce a gun, Zac poked his finger gun harder, looked him in the eye, and said "Slowly".

"Woah man, I'm just reaching for my ID."

"With one hand, carefully open your jacket, and with the other hand, I want you to pinch your finger and thumb together, and pull out your ID," Zac said with a stern look on his face. "Any sudden moves and I will shoot."

Upon hearing this, Mike carefully and with deliberate movements peeled open his jacket and produced his ID.

He slowly unfolded the leather wallet and showed a shiny metal badge and warrant card.

"I'm the same as you man, I'm in the job, so put your weapon away and I will stick the kettle on."

Relieved, Zac stood up.

"I'm undercover for my brother."

"Good to hear. I had cause to come here, because I heard

Colby and Tommy plotting against you, and I wanted to make sure you were okay."

Mike squinted his eyes at Zac and he lowered the gun, slowly releasing the hammer on the pistol.

"There's something about you... have we met?".

"A long time ago, I was at Zac's 9th birthday party."

"That must be it," said Mike, putting the gun away. "Sorry about slamming you on the floor."

He reached a hand out to Zac and pulled him up. Zac rubbed his side.

"That's okay, pretty good moves you've got there".

Mike made a couple of hot drinks, and they chatted about the 9th birthday party and talked about what had happened since.

"It's weird, I am not usually like this, but I feel like I've known you my entire life, like a good friend I never had," said Mike.

Zac smiled.

"I'm not a cop, my brother's the family police officer, he just wanted me to do some undercover for him, like a confidential informant, and he knew that my time in the service would be helpful."

Zac listened as his father carried on talking.

"There had been chatter that something big was going to happen, and we needed to get me in to find out more information because my brother is already known to them, but they don't know me. That way we could get Tommy and Colby to give up the boss, and foil the plan, although we still don't know what the plan is yet."

"They plan to blow the dam, and kill everyone, and we've got to stop them. But we have intelligence that says that they aren't the people at the top, and we want to catch the ringleader," said Zac.

"What? That's unbelievable... how do you know this?"

"My department has been gathering intelligence for years,

and we are convinced there is a criminal mastermind behind all this," Zac replied, not wanting to give himself away as a time traveller.

"He's never contacted me though. Guess I wasn't trusted enough. I wondered if they had worked out who I was a while back but wasn't sure." Mike replied

"I got the feeling that they knew, Tommy seems disgruntled because you're always ordering him around, and Colby has aspirations of being the Mayor of Kisterwich, so he's willing to do anything to get you out of the way," Zac said.

"Right, that's it. This has gone too far now, time to go get 'em" said Mike, putting his gun in his belt, and his badge in his pocket.

CHAPTER 29

Zac got into the passenger seat of his dad's car, and Mike drove the convertible, heading towards the cinema.

"There's a back way in, we can go through there and surprise them," said Mike.

"Sounds like a plan," replied Zac.

They went behind the building, avoiding the car park.

They both got out of the car, and Zac waited while Mike unlocked the backroom doors.

The place was quiet, and after about ten minutes of looking, there were no signs of Tommy and Colby.

Mike picked up the phone and put it on speakerphone.

"Tommy, where are you?"

"Just grabbing a bite to eat boss, and Colby has gone somewhere. He didn't say where." He munched on his sandwich, then speaking with his mouth full said, "Do you need us, Boss?"

"No, that's fine, just take the rest of the day off," replied Mike.

"Oh, thanks Boss," said Tommy, practically smiling down the phone.

"Are you okay? You're not usually-,"

Mike interrupted, "I'm not usually what?"

"Er, nothing Boss,"

"Go, before I change my mind," replied Mike.

Tommy closed his flip phone, ending the call.

"That's not like Colby to go somewhere without telling me, I wonder what his game is."

"Perhaps your cover is blown?" Zac asked.

Mike rubbed his mouth and chin in thought.

"If your cover is blown, what would be his next course of action?" Asked Zac.

"I've read his file. Unlike Tommy, he has methods and is very clinical. Tommy is just sloppy, but Colby always gets the job done."

"So, if he saw you as a threat to the plan, he would do what?"

"He'd go after my family, so there is no one to ask questions, then he would come after me."

Mike's face tensed up, and he tightened his fists, his knuckles turning white.

"My son, that sicko would go after Zac. We have to get to the school and get him to safety."

———

The car screeched to a halt outside the school.

"I don't know which classroom he's in," said Mike.

"Go to the headteacher's office and ask. Tell them he's got an emergency doctor's appointment or something." Zac pointed down the corridor. "I'm going to check down there and look in all the windows, to see if I can find him. If I do, I will bring him to the head's office."

Mike walked towards the headmaster's office, while Zac headed straight to the classroom he remembered being in that day, all those years ago.

As he walked up to the door, he mentally prepared himself. Inside that classroom, was a younger version of Zac, all his classmates, and the teacher he needed desperately to talk to.

There was only one thing for it.

He looked at the door and hesitated. The black letters on the fuzzy classroom window lettering read 'Ms Diane Northek'. He knocked on the door.

"Come in" came a voice from within.

He opened the door and looked straight at her, and at that moment, he realised that the mysterious man who interrupted the boring lesson that day was himself, from the future.

"Ms Northek, I need to speak to you, it's urgent."

She got up from her chair and walked to the door. "Darren Black, you're in charge until I get back".

Closing the door, she asked, "What's this about, I have a class to teach, and my time is important to these children."

"My name is Agent Santelle, and I work for the government." Zac started. "We have been placed on a level five alert after a terrorist was seen at the dam this morning, and we need to get you all to safety fast."

Diane shuffled her feet, looked him straight in the eye and asked, "What do you want me to do?"

Recounting the events of that day in his head, he knew what was going to happen, and told her to stay put.

"You need to stay in your classroom, with the children, and wait. We have the army involved, and your main hall is being used as a temporary hospital. The children will be called when their parents arrive."

"My husband, will he be alright?" She asked.

"You can count on it". He said with a smile.

She thanked him and closed the door, and Zac walked down the corridor to the caretaker's closet, opened the door, and waited inside for what was going to happen next.

Within minutes, the bell had gone, and he heard lots of children leaving their classrooms ready to meet up with their parents.

Sometime later, the noise quietened, and the last steps of the children became silent as they emptied the corridor. Zac opened the closet door and crossed the hallway into the classroom.

When he was younger, he had always sat in the same chair, two rows back, and on the end near the door.

His pencils and pens were all still on the desk along with the exercise book, as young Zac had left them when he went to the toilet, expecting to come back to the classroom. He opened the younger Zac's schoolbag and found the journal. He was looking through the book when Zac heard Mike shouting.

"Zac, Zac!". The door opened, and Zac quickly put the book behind his back.

"Ah, Agent Santelle, I guess you haven't found him yet either."

"Yes, he's in the hall, surrounded by lots of people. The nurse has just taken him to see his mum." Replied Zac.

"Good, now let's find Tommy and Colby before they blow up the dam."

CHAPTER 30

Tommy looked up from the chair, waiting patiently to be called.

"Tommy Collins to see Dr Jo Sunae in room 3 please." Tommy limped into the doctor's office.

Colby was still in the waiting room when his phone rang. The LCD readout said, Unknown Caller.

The receptionist called out, "Sorry, you can't answer that in here, you need to go outside,"

From the doctor's office window, Tommy could see Colby outside talking on his phone.

"Hello?" Colby stood up, straighter than usual, and an expression of respect shone across his face, as if he were with a loved relative, and were expected to do his best at all times.

"Yes sir, of course sir." He listened more. After approximately one minute, he said goodbye and ended the call.

Colby sat back in the waiting room, and Tommy walked out of the office with a crutch underneath each arm.

Colby looked at him, and Tommy stuck his leg out.

"Two stitches," he said, hobbling out of the hospital's entrance.

"That was Mr Devander. There is a change of plan." Colby told Tommy.

"Mr Devander? He never calls. It must be important." Replied Tommy. "What did he say?".

"It appears that our boss is a police officer."

"I knew that guy was a flippin' cop. I said it all along," replied Tommy with a smug grin.

Colby preened his moustache.

"So come on then, what are the new orders?" Asked Tommy.

"You, my friend, finally get to kill him." He said looking at the fat man.

Tommy smiled with a menacing grin, looking at the wound in his leg. "Good!"

"And then we get to blame his wife for the bombing."

"I always wondered why he was hired in the first place." Tommy shook his head. "I knew he was a cop, just knew it."

They got into the car and headed towards the cinema. Tommy pulled the slide back on his gun, popping a round in the chamber.

They had almost reached the cinema when they drove past Mike's convertible. Tommy stuck his gun out of the rear passenger window and fired at Mike's vehicle.

"Looks like your cover is blown," said Zac as Mike put his foot down on the pedal. Colby's skilful driving spun Tommy's car into a sharp u-turn, and as dust, rubber and grit filled the air, the wheels spun and the car shot forward.

The mirror shook and vibrated, and all Mike saw was the yellow of Tommy's car. The sound of bullets got louder the closer they got. Colby had his foot down to the floor, and the engine growled as they crunched bumpers together.

Zac's seat jerked, and he looked back to see the car now moving to get beside them. Tommy had moved over from one side of the car's back seat to the other side, and the window was now down, ready to shoot again. Bullets whizzed through the air, shattering the side windows of the other car, and making holes in the side doors.

"You're dead, both of yer" shouted Tommy as he pulled the trigger again. At that moment, Colby hit a bump in the road, and Tommy dropped his gun. It clattered out of the car and onto the road and was lost in the dust and debris behind them in seconds.

Colby shouted, "Get your arm in and buckle up". The engine growled, and Colby smashed straight into Zac and Mike, busting up the wing mirror, and messing up the body-work down the side of their car.

Both cars raced side by side for a while, and as Colby pushed closer to Mike, Mike reacted by pulling away.

A sign whizzed by, showing a sharp corner in 100 yards.

"Their car is much heavier than ours, we won't take much more of that," said Mike. "Hang on, I have a plan." He braked hard.

In a mere moment, there was a look of dread and confusion on Tommy's face, as Tommy's car shot past, and as Colby took the bend hard, the car rolled over and into the ditch at the corner.

The car was upside down, there was blood on Colby's face, his tie was draped downwards and Tommy was feeling sick. There was a knock on the door, and Mike shouted "Police, You're under arrest".

————

The metal bars clanged on the cell, and Mike locked the door.

Graham walked up to Tommy and Colby, eyeing them up and down.

"Who on earth do you think you are?" he said, his thick Scottish accent filling the air.

"You think you can come to *my* town and plan something like this? I demand you to tell me where Mr Devander is. If you tell us, I will be lenient on you and tell the judge you co-operated with the investigation.".

"And what happens if we don't?" Said Tommy, trying to call his bluff.

Graham tapped the barrel of his gun against the bars of the cell and whispered, "Well… Let's put it this way. I don't think you want to be here when the Dam floods the town, do you?"

"You can't do that, you're the cops. You've got rules."

Colby stood up off the bunk and looked at Graham. "I've seen that look before, he's not lying."

Graham smiled.

"So, what would it take to let us out of here? Your police-man's wage can't pay enough for all of this. Wouldn't you rather retire and kick back? How does fifty thousand sound?"

Graham pulled back the hammer on his gun. "I'm not for sale."

"Oh jeez, he ain't kidding around man," said Tommy.

"Shut up" retorted Colby.

"I don't know where he is. The last time we met him, it was at the back of the Corderdale Apartments, on the bottom floor in the car park at the back."

Colby punched Tommy hard, and Tommy went down like a sack of spuds.

"What was that for?" Tommy asked rubbing his jaw.

"You just cost me my boat."

CHAPTER 31

Graham moved back to the desk and picked up the phone. "Get me the Army."

While Graham chatted on the phone, explaining the situation, Mike told a police officer to take the two men to Newhaven PD, in a secure prisoner transport van.

"I'm off to the Corderdale Apartments, anyone coming with me?" Asked Zac, grabbing the loudhailer.

"I'm going to stay here with Graham, you need to get that guy, I will meet you there as soon as we have moved these two," said Mike handing him a gun "You're going to need this."

———

Zac reached the Apartments. They were in the posh part of town and buildings rose high in a large block like the sort of thing you would see at a luxury holiday resort. Each one had a balcony, satellite TV, and solar panels. They were very high-end.

He held the loudhailer to his mouth and shouted, "Mr

Devander, my name is Agent Santelle from the Government. You're surrounded. Come out with your hands up."

Zac pulled the gun out of his pocket.

Two figures walked slowly towards him, and he recognised his brother's silhouette before he got halfway to him. Mr Devander was holding a gun behind him.

"What are you doing here?" Shouted Zac with a confused tone.

"I went to get you help when you went into the cave, and he grabbed me." He said.

The man spoke in a gravelly voice. "Drop the gun, or I drop your brother," said the man. There was a pause, and the gun clattered at Zac's feet.

"So, this is the great Mr Devander... inventor of the ID Fob, Luminettes, and Holovision? Honestly man, what happened to you?".

"I made much more than that. Over 92% of the world's tech was created by me, including the time travel tech that enabled you to be here."

"You've got it so good, why do you want to blow up the dam?"

He walked closer to Zac, and Zac looked straight at him.

"Hey, I know you. You look older, but it's you. You're Oliver Black, the security guard at the dam."

"What have you done with Mr Devander, you maniac?".

"Don't you get it... There is no Mr Devander. He's not real. Even the name isn't real. It's short for Development And Experimental Research."

"Dev And ER" repeated Zac, the penny dropping.

"All of this was to get the money up to exact my revenge and kill everyone in Kisterwich."

"But why?"

"Zac" shouted Rhea from behind Oliver and his brother.

Oliver turned around, Dylan punched him, and he dropped the gun. He kicked the gun away. Going for another swing, he missed, and Oliver made a run for it, towards the supermarket.

Zac fired the pistol until the gun was empty, missing every time. Frustrated, he threw the gun on the floor and went over to Dylan to check he was okay.

"Let's get him" shouted Rhea.

Zac ran into the car park, closely followed by Rhea and Dylan.

CHAPTER 32

"He's going into the supermarket" shouted Dylan, as they all diverged onto his location.

"Dylan, you cut him off at the door, and I will grab him" shouted Rhea running from the right-hand side of the car park.

Oliver tried the supermarket's front door, but it didn't budge.

Spotting the old telephone box, he made a run for it.

Zac saw him change course and shouted, "he's going for the phone box".

Dylan was the first to arrive at the old red box and pulled on the door to open it. It was stuck fast, with the evil man inside it, a wide grin on his face.

By the time Rhea arrived, Zac and Dylan were both pulling on the telephone box.

"Ha! Now we've got you" said Zac with a triumphant look on his face as the door opened, and they grabbed him.

Oliver looked at Rhea, smiling even more than before.

"How can you just stand there and grin?" Scowled Rhea.

Zac had never seen this angry side of Rhea before, and it made him admire her even more.

"I know what happens next," replied Oliver with a chuckle.

Dylan looked him in the eye, "Okay, you've got my attention, what happens next?"

Oliver opened his mouth to speak, and paused, then closed it.

"Didn't think so," said Dylan with a confident look in his eye. "We got you fair and square, and you're just trying to psych us all out. It will not work this time."

"What I want to know is why?" Asked Zac "Why do you want to blow up the dam, kill all those people, and blame it all on my mother?"

"I'd like to know that too," said Dylan, with an angry tone.

The wind fell silent, and Oliver started to explain.

"I was born here you know, in Kisterwich." Started Oliver "And I went to the school in Newhaven."

Zac, Dylan and Rhea listened, wondering where this was going.

"I was a child prodigy, the best in the school, and the teachers knew it. They said one day, that I was going to be the best in my field." He looked downward at the floor.

"Except for one teacher, your father," he said as he looked at Zac.

"Hey, he's my father too," said Dylan.

"I came up with many brilliant ideas. Most of the tech you use were my inventions."

"That's a load of crap," said Rhea angrily. "Those are my Uncles ideas."

"Those ideas are over 30 years old, most of them I submitted as homework while I attended school," said Oliver "I submitted them all in the two years I was doing my last exams, and all to your father, he said looking at Zac. But after your father made sure I failed, and my assignments received low grades, I realised something else was happening."

So, one day, I dropped my work onto your father's desk, after I had been in his class. I waited outside at the tennis courts overlooking the teacher's car park, and sure enough, a man arrived. It wasn't your dad though; it was the head teacher, and he had a wallet full of papers. Wondering how I was going to follow him when he drove off, I was quite surprised when an army car pulled up next to his car. The man got out and chatted to the head teacher, and then gave him a large brown envelope, with a thick wad of something inside... I can only assume it was cash, and in return, he got my papers. Just to be sure, I repeated the same thing the following week, only this time I had a camera.

When I confronted him, he just laughed, told me I was making it all up and called me a liar. Worse still, when I approached your father, he flatly denied it, and told me, "even if I did what you're accusing me of, who would believe me anyway?".

"Shortly after that, my grades fell even more, and I was kicked out for poor work standards. I vowed one day I would clear my name and get back from your father what he stole from me! I later found out he had gambling problems, and it all finally made sense."

"Wait, so you're saying that you gave the work to my dad, and the head sold it? That's not our dad's fault he sold it." Shouted Dylan.

"So you just thought you would kill everyone?" Zac asked.

"Well, it seemed like a good idea at the time."

"You are insane!" Exclaimed Zac.

"Insanity is defined as doing the same thing repeatedly and expecting different results. What I have done is change what I needed to do, to get different results. And now, I intend to kill you."

Dylan looked at Oliver with a confused look on his face and asked, "You and whose army?"

A voice behind them shouted, "This Army."

They all turned around. Behind them was a vast crowd walking slowly into the car park. As they came closer, Dylan looked to see who they were. Zac squinted to get a good look too.

"Last chance, give up Zac Drummond, and let Oliver go, and you can both leave unharmed, or prepare to fight." Shouted a voice from the crowd.

The crowd inched closer, and the hairs on Zac's neck prickled with fear.

"Never," shouted Dylan "I left him once, I will not leave him again."

The crowd drew in further, and Rhea noticed the same features in each crowd member.

She turned to Oliver "You are crazy".

"Rhea, what's going on?" Asked Zac.

"Look at the faces," she trembled.

Zac squinted.

"What? That's not possible!" Exclaimed Dylan "They are all... him!"

CHAPTER 33

The crowd had now surrounded the telephone box, and all their faces were recognisable. They did all look like Oliver in some respects, but there were differences.

Some were wearing different clothes, one had different coloured eyes, one had almost translucent skin, another had short hair, the one at the back was blonde, and another a redhead.

One had bucked teeth, another had a striped complexion that made him look almost like a zebra. Each one of the crowd had discernible differences, but they all looked the same, they all looked like Oliver.

The telephone box door opened and Oliver got out.

"STOP!" Shouted Oliver.

The crowd came to a standstill.

"Attention." Each clone stood up straight and slapped the arms to their sides with their chins up.

"Meet my time clones," he said with a big grin on his face.

"They're not much to look at, but they are all me, and they all do what I tell them to do. I used the machine and realised there was a flaw… each clone would only last 4 hours before cellular cohesion failed and they would turn into soup. More improvements later, and you have what you see before you."

"You call these improvements?" Rhea retorted. "These are failures, not one of them is a clone. What have you done to make these any better? All you've done is create monsters."

"Every single one of these clones lasts years, not just hours… so I can have all sorts of fun messing with the time streams, and now that my army is up and running, I intend to get rid of you lot and then use my time clones to alter history, so that I am never seen as a failure ever again, and I will get what's rightfully mine… a place in the history books as the best scientist of all time!".

"And how are you going to do that?" Asked Dylan.

"Easy, each clone has been born with the same nanotech inside it that allows me to voice control them. I can get them to do anything I want,". He grinned, rubbing his hands. "And right now, I want them to get rid of you all,"

Zac hesitated "But you said you just want me, and you would let my friends go."

"That was before I told you my plan, but now you all know, I can't just let them walk away now.. can I?".

Dylan turned to Rhea "What does that mean?"

Zac looked at Oliver and said, "It means he's going to kill us". He looked for confirmation.

"Not me" Oliver pointed to the crowd, panning it from left to right. "Them".

Silence fell.

Oliver was the first one to break the silence.

"Kill them!"

CHAPTER 34

Rhea's gaze at Oliver dropped as the clones moved in. The striped clone was the first to strike. Rhea ran in, fists waving and screaming. Stripeys' feet thudded against the floor. He lashed out with a skilful blow and glanced across Dylan's face. Dylan spun around, and half dazed lashed out with his arms, attempting to hit the first thing he saw.

Unfortunately for him, Zac was the first thing that Dylan's fists contacted. In a slow-motion wobble, the skin across Zac's face rippled as it temporarily enveloped Dylan's fist.

"Woah, that hurt" screamed Zac, and he ducked as another fist came towards him, this time from another clone.

Meanwhile, Rhea was taking on four at once. Her karate moves were sending them flying as she did sidekicks, and punches and clones were being pushed out of her way, in the same way, that pins went down after being hit by a bowling ball.

Dylan stood completely gob-smacked as she kicked and punched clone after clone, in a relentless pursuit of perfection, almost as if she was going for a trophy at the end of this. He felt she was worthy of a medal or something.

Another clone hurtled towards Zac. This one had spotted skin and striped hair, and Zac wondered what on earth must have been wrong with the CellPrint to create such a misfit. The spiked hair made this clone look taller and scarier, but the fact that he had picked up a pipe and was swinging it at Zac made him look terrifying. The pipe came within inches of his legs, and Zac jumped clear of it before it could knock his legs from beneath him.

Dylan, completely in awe with the spectacle of Rheas fighting didn't see the foot from the long-haired clone with three legs, and as it hit him in the stomach, he felt himself buckle under his weight as he collapsed to the floor, all the wind knocked out of him.

"Noooooooo!" Shouted Zac as he pushed through the crowd in a futile attempt to help his brother. It was pointless though, as pointless as a fish climbing a tree.

Dylan lay on the floor helpless, dribbling, and looking upwards as the three-legged freak was smacked in the face by the cross-eyed clone who stood next to him.

"Oops," said cross-eyes sarcastically, who ended up eating a fist from three-legs, with a big smile on his face.

Stripey laughed as cross-eyes went down to the floor, and Rhea seized the opportunity to bang Stripey straight on the nose, and he joined the pile of clones on the floor, knocked out cold.

"Yea, how d'you like those apples?" Called out Dylan as he got to his feet.

Oliver looked on and laughed as he watched what was going on. His clone minions were no match for their three opponents, although Rhea was giving them a run for their money.

The clones surrounded Rhea in a big circle and were egging each other on to fight her.

"Go on, she's just a girl," said a short one to a green clone.

"You've gotta be kidding me," came the reply.

One big beefy guy came through the crowd, and a line parted, letting him through.

Zac looked at Dylan. "We need to help, otherwise she's toast," he said.

The Beefy clone opened his mouth and gave a roar that made Dylan jump.

"You're mine," he said in a high-pitched voice.

Zac coughed and laughed at the same time, the Beefy guy's voice catching him by surprise.

His face went red with anger, as the rage built up inside him, and he pushed forward, knocking clones left and right like a bowling ball, flattening a bunch of pins when you hit a strike, as he barged through them.

Rhea stood her ground and watched as he stopped. Dylan, now back on his feet, called out "Get out of there Rhea". Her gaze was fixed on the beefy guy as he beat his muscled chest, then launched forwards towards her.

Another slow-motion moment, as the sounds became deeper and slower, fists and legs moved at a tenth of the speed, and Beefy's speed had reduced as he reached Rhea. In a fraction of a second, Beefy launched across the room. His body slowly left the ground, and with arms stretched it felt like several seconds for him to reach her.

He watched and shouted. The sounds left his lips like a guttural war cry, too slow to be heard by human ears, all the time calling "Noooooooooo".

Just as Beefys fist touched Rheas' hair, her coordinated body sensed his oncoming attack; she ducked onto one knee, and as his body flew past her head, she reached up with a fist, right in the family jewels.

Time sped up, and in the next moment Beefy was doubled in pain on the floor behind Rhea, with the Professor's Assistant knelt on the floor on one leg, her fist raised, and her head held high.

Dylan blinked and missed it all.

"Get off me you idiot" shouted a voice. Beneath the pile of hurting clones was Oliver flattened by the big man. He pushed Beefy aside and shouted, "Get me out of here".

Several clones grabbed his arms, as others made a path through the crowd, and they picked Oliver up and ushered him to safety.

Oliver pointed at Rhea, Dylan and Zac.

"Kill them!"

Dylan looked around him. There were clones everywhere. He was tired from fighting, and there was no way they were going to win this. Zac was drained of energy too, and Rhea was only fighting two clones at once, instead of the four at the beginning of the brawl, so it wouldn't be too long before she was done.

Zac, seeing the desperation on his brother's face, and their impending loss, dropped to his knees in sheer exhaustion and was about to give himself to the crowd of clones when something quite unexpected happened.

Dylan thrust his fist in the air, grasping something.

"Look what I found," he said, holding up the nano gun.

"Rhea, you're our best bet," shouted Dylan.

He looked at Zac "Sorry bro, but we have to be realistic about this."

His brother made a gesture to show he was okay with it.

Rhea carried on, not listening. She was completely in the zone, mustering up all the energy she could, to fight the two clones she was battling.

Oliver grinned.

"And what are you going to do with that? They are all under my voice control," he said.

Zac stood up, narrowly missing a swinging fist, and ducking as another foot came towards his face.

Rhea had finished fighting her clones now and shouted out, "What did you find Dylan?"

He waved his arm with the gun in it, and she pushed through the crowd towards him.

Rhea was almost within several feet when a clone kicked the gun out of Dylan's hands, and he dropped it onto the floor.

"Ha!" said Oliver, with a look of complete glee on his face.

"Zac, can you reach your brother?" shouted Rhea. He attempted to go forward towards Dylan but was thrown to the floor, and ended up at the bottom of a pile of clones, all pummelling him.

Dylan lost sight of Zac, and the gun and all he could see was Rhea, now within arm's reach, and what seemed like an enormous sea of clones, with wave upon wave of them surging forwards.

As Rhea reached Dylan, more attackers unexpectedly parted in a large 360-degree ripple, knocking each other flat, and Zac stood up high, with the gun in his hand as they all lay dazed, completely surprised by what had just happened.

The sudden rush of adrenalin from picking up the gun was enough to turn him into one of these superhuman types he had seen on TV.

He looked at the gun's LCD readout; *only two bullets left.* Aiming the weapon at Oliver, he pulled the trigger. The bullet flew across the room. It whizzed past stripey, three-legs, beefy, the girl clone, and hundreds of others, and Dylan, Zac, and Rhea watched with anticipation as it flew through the air. It smashed on the wall behind Oliver and became a million pieces, disintegrating into a small dust cloud.

"Try again" Rhea called out.

Closing one eye, he held the pistol up and squeezed gently. There was hardly any recoil, and the bullet hit the target straight away.

"And what do you expect to do now?" Asked Oliver.

"Stop moving" shouted Zac.

He thought for a moment and then issued a second order.

"Now repeat after me… I want all clones to stop fighting and stand to attention."

Oliver's face dropped, as the nanobots got to work on his nervous system, attaching themselves to his brain, and leaving him completely at the mercy of the orders that Zac had given him.

"I want all clones to stop fighting and stand to attention," called out Oliver.

Immediately, and in unison, the entire troop came to a halt, and each clone stood ready, chins up, chest out, arms by their side, and feet together, waiting for their next orders, except for the one with green hair, who fell over, and planked on the floor.

"Keep fighting" called out Oliver.

"Shut up" ordered Zac.

Oliver went silent, and the look on his face dropped even more.

"Now… Repeat the order I just gave you,"

Once more the clones came to attention, and the whole place became silent.

"Finally, I was getting a headache," said Dylan.

"Now repeat this… safety protocols off."

Without any hesitation, Oliver begrudgingly repeated the order, and all the clones shouted "safety protocols off".

Now tell them to self-terminate.

Oliver called out the order, and within seconds each clone started to dissolve. Some dissolved straight away with a splash, as if a water balloon had burst, and some more slowly, with limbs dropping off at the joints, like zombies who had reached their expiration date. Within a minute, everywhere around them was a sea of red goo, with the odd strand of green hair, and only Rhea, Zac, Dylan, and Oliver were left standing. The room smelled of the sweet smell of bacon. Zac watched Oliver, ready to give the next order, but he didn't have to. Oliver was already melting into puddles from the feet upwards as if he was made of metal and had stepped into hot Lava.

Dylan watched as Oliver's feet disappeared, and gravity pulled Oliver downwards. His ankles were next, then his knees. An arm dropped off and splashed into liquid as it hit the floor, and Oliver looked at it in horror, knowing there was nothing he could do about it.

"You can talk now," said Zac.

"Any last words?" Asked Rhea.

"You haven't won, and you haven't seen the last of me," replied Oliver.

What remained of his body exploded, spraying ovine DNA everywhere, and Rhea, Dylan, and Zac all got covered in the sludge.

Dylan looked at Zac and high-fived him, smiling at each other.

"I suppose I have to clear this lot up?" Asked Dylan.

"Nah, let someone else do it, we need to get Dad," replied Zac with a grin.

CHAPTER 35

The toilet flushed, and the words "Historical Change Occurred" came over the speakers in the lab.

Zac opened the door, still doing up his flies, and said, "Really? You couldn't wait until I was out of there?".

"There have been some enormous changes", said the Professor. His viewscreen played the video of the last jump, and Zac watched eagerly.

By the time the video had finished, he was happy that everything had worked out, all he wanted to do was go home and give his family a big hug.

But there was a nagging doubt somewhere in the back of his head.

"What about other evidence? DNA and other forensics?" He asked the Professor.

"It's confirmed. The DNA matches that of Oliver Black."

"But what about the woman in the car who forced my mum to blow up the dam originally?".

"Files show, that the Kisterwich Police Department found the car and used enhanced techniques to pull evidence from the vehicle after the flood damage." The Holoprof paused for a moment while it accessed more information. "The DNA in the back of the car matched Oliver Black, and it was concluded in the investigation that hair fibres also found in the car came from a woman's wig."

"Are you saying that Oliver Black dressed up as a woman to fool us?"

"Precisely Zac, and it seemed to fool everyone except the forensics lab."

Zac smiled, then breathed an enormous sigh of relief.

"So then, the dam is safe, all the people of Kisterwich are safe, and so are my family. That's a job well done."

"There is the matter of that one more mission, Zac. After all, I've kept up my end of the bargain."

"Of course. I understand. Destroy Latimer, let's do this." he said with a sad look in his eye. He walked over to the TripleScan, laid down, and pressed the button one final time.

———

Zac woke up. He walked into the computer room, watched the CCTV cameras for a moment, and then switched on the TV. The news started up, and Zac smiled as he saw the intro with its typical view above the town, and the sun shining on the water in the reservoir. Everything was just great.

Following the procedure that the Professor had given him, he started the shutdown sequence. In the computer suite, all the hard drives wiped themselves, and with the programming erased, there was nothing to keep the safety protocols working. The capacitor hummed loudly, then it got rather warm inside the lab, and as Zac reached the exit doors, he heard the capacitor overloading with a high-pitched whine as it split apart. The resulting overload sent an electrical surge back through the internal power grid frying all the computers, the Cellprint, and Triplescan.

With the whole place irreversibly destroyed, Zac walked out of the lab and up to the top of Appleton Hill. He lay down on the grass and watched as the sun rose.

He smiled, then melted into a bacon puddle.

CHAPTER 36

year after his first time-jump, Zac and his brother were visiting their parents for a family dinner.

He poured some wine into everyone's glasses.

"I have some splendid news to share. After the robbery at the museum, their insurance paid up, and the amount they are going to pay me will be more than enough to pay for a lifetime license with the PHPC."

"Does that mean you don't have to worry about that pesky bill anymore?" Asked his brother.

"Precisely. Of course, it means I will never see my journal again, but that means I can afford to keep Libros Antiques open."

They clapped. "At least something good came out of it", his dad said while chomping on some potatoes.

After dinner, Zac poured out some more wine, then switched on the Holovision to watch The Amnesty.

"Dad, are you coming?" Asked Dylan.

"Just finished filling the sonowasher, I'm on my way now," he said as he entered the living room. He sat down on the settee next to Rebecca, and they watched the end of the news.

"And our last article tonight is about the infamous paper

journal robbery from the Museum de Monde in Newhaven last year. The police have concluded their investigation into the red-haired woman spotted at the scene and said that she has still never been found. The investigation has now been shelved, and the woman is still at large … for now. This is Brent Jastock and Kit Gersairy reporting for News Show Live. Thanks for watching and stay safe."

Dylan leaned over to Zac and whispered, "Now we know who left the journal in the shop."

Dylan and Zac both looked at each other and mouthed the name, Rhea.

Rebecca stood up and raised her glass.

"Happy Birthday, Zac."

They all raised their glasses in celebration, "Cheers".

SHOW YOUR SUPPORT

If you enjoyed this book, why not leave me a review so other people can enjoy this book as well? Reviews help independent Authors like me, to get our books out to other readers, and your review will mean a lot to me.

Want to know more about my books?
You can check out my website
https://www.brettishbooks.com

Join the mailing list
https://www.brettishbooks.com/signup

Join me on social media.
Facebook: https://www.facebook.com/groups/brettishbooks
Twitter: https://twitter.com/brettishbooks

ABOUT THE AUTHOR

My name is Brett Jackson, and I run BrettishBooks.com.

I have been writing seriously (during the pandemic) since September 2020 and officially opened BrettishBooks in April 2021 .

After starting this book 4 and a half years earlier, (by writing it in my spare time) I started to take my Author career seriously. I now have a dedicated writing space, and a specific time throughout the week.

It wasn't always like that though. One period in my life, I refused to write, I was... the writer who wouldn't, but I had no problems with typing, so that was okay :)

It helps when you write about things you love, and I am really into Science Fiction, Time Travel, anything with aliens, the future, poetry (where did that come from???) and more.

For most of my life, I have been into gadgets, computers, and my family (I even ran a successful business, fixing and building computers).

Lately, however, since the children have all grown up, and left home, I have regained my love of reading, and that's when I got into writing.

As part of my writing skill base, I am also studying as a copywriter and editor to level up my knowledge as a writer.

When I am not on the website or writing my book, I am on social media with other authors or enjoying life with my wife and family.

Please join me, as I carry on levelling up as an Author, and go from writing my first novel (this book) to my dream of becoming a best seller... not for the money (although that's a bonus), or for the fame (as if that's going to happen), but for the satisfaction of being able to prove to myself that I could do it, and to stir your emotions and imagination, as you climb into the worlds I create.

Thanks for your support.

– Brett Jackson.

Printed in Great Britain
by Amazon

30799288R00119